"I'm looking for a man."

Ian's eyes dropped to Natasha's sling, then bulky walking boot. "This guy responsible for all that?" He motioned to the injuries.

Fury flashed in her expression and Lexi stiffened. A low growl rumbled from the dog's throat.

Ian froze. He did *not* want those teeth sinking into his hide.

"It's okay, girl," Natasha whispered, her left hand stroking the black fur. "We've been together for four years. She senses my moods and interprets my body language, then responds accordingly."

"She going to bite me if you get mad?" He'd have to rethink his strategy on making the woman go home.

"Only if I give her the command." Natasha's lips quirked. "Or if I'm unconscious and she thinks you're a threat."

"Good to know." He swallowed, doing his best to radiate harmless vibes. "The man you're searching for, did he give you those injuries?"

"Yes."

"And you're going after him? By yourself?"

P.A. DePaul resides outside Philadelphia in the US. In her free time, you can find her reading, working on a puzzle, playing with her dog, winning game nights against her husband (sometimes) or whipping up something in the kitchen. You can learn more about her at padepaul.com, Facebook.com/padepaul and Instagram.com/padepaul.

Visit the Author Profile page at LoveInspired.com.

Surviving Alaska

P.A. DePaul

LOVE INSPIRED
INSPIRATIONAL ROMANCE

LOVE INSPIRED®

INSPIRATIONAL ROMANCE

ISBN-13: 978-1-335-55596-0

Recycling programs
for this product may
not exist in your area.

Surviving Alaska

Copyright © 2023 by Penni DePaul

For questions and comments about the quality of this book, please contact us
at CustomerService@Harlequin.com.

Love Inspired
22 Adelaide St. West, 41st Floor
Toronto, Ontario M5H 4E3, Canada
www.LoveInspired.com

Printed in U.S.A.

But the wicked are like the troubled sea, when it cannot rest, whose waters cast up mire and dirt.
—*Isaiah* 57:20

This book is dedicated to K-9 heroes and heroines everywhere. Thank you for your amazing service.

Acknowledgments

A huge thank-you goes to my husband. He's a sounding board, brainstormer and rock star at keeping the household running while I'm writing.

Massive squishy hugs go to my agent, Michelle Grajkowski, and editor, Johanna Raisanen. I love you both!

I don't even know where to begin on the thank-you scale for Rich Worthington and the Lower Moreland Police Department. Rich, thank you for allowing me to use your name. Hopefully you're okay with becoming an ASAC with the FBI. :) Thank you for answering my litany of emails, calls, texts and popping in the station. You rule. I own every mistake and stretch of reality.

My final thank-you belongs to you, the reader. I appreciate the support and your time in reading this labor of love. It means the world to me.

Chapter One

Lexi whined, her pitch starting with a high complaint and ending on a low growl.

Natasha Greene transferred a worthless tissue into her right hand, which was dangling from a sling, and buried her fingers between the German shepherd's pointed ears. She silently agreed with the assessment.

Yesterday, they had spent seventeen tedious, and painful, hours locked inside airports and planes, thanks to layovers and delays. Landing too late at night in Anchorage, they had shared a budget hotel room, then, this morning, hopped onto a small charter plane flying northwest, hauling mail and supplies.

She needed the brief reprieve on solid ground. And yet...

The village of Whisper, Alaska—population 436—couldn't be more opposite from Philadelphia if it tried. Tucked into the heart of the untamed interior, basic infrastructure such as highways didn't exist. Like most of the state, the village was isolated and only accessible by small planes.

Within Whisper, mud strips simulated roads while colorful homes comprised of wood and scavenged materials were in desperate need of repair. Rusty wires penned chickens but uncollared dogs roamed free. The only asphalt found was at the airport. And calling the single patchwork building an "airport" was generous. The structure pulled triple duty as a terminal, warehouse, and hangar.

But the view surrounding the locals could not be beat. In the distance, majestic mountains and flourishing forests stretched for miles.

A strong gust of wind snatched at Natasha's baseball cap and clanged metal signs, clinging for survival on rusty bolts, against the terminal.

Summer had decided to skip this part of Alaska, or gave up and let fall have its way. Instead of shorts and tank tops for August, Natasha needed a coat and gloves. Great. She had hoped the internet had lied when she researched what to pack for the trip. It hadn't.

Another gust iced through her lightweight jacket and tactical pants.

"Dalton's around here somewhere," the charter pilot, Skip, interrupted her survey. "We're meetin' for lunch."

For the first time since she left Philadelphia International Airport, Natasha doubted her plan. In her mind, it had seemed so simple. But now…

"Head on inside," the pilot yelled over his shoulder as he strode toward an open hangar bay. "It'll be warmer." He pointed at a dirty glass door at the front of the building.

Peering into Lexi's big brown eyes, Natasha prayed she hadn't made the second worst mistake of her life.

Ian Dalton tossed the saturated rag on top of the growing pile inside a broken laundry basket. Grabbing another from the warped cardboard box, he dropped the piece of old T-shirt onto the floor of his aging Cessna 180.

"Never again," he muttered, attacking the red berry liquid seeping into the crevasses. The old man and young kid on his earlier flight had refused to listen. Ian had told them repeatedly they shouldn't hold the large beverage cooler. He offered to strap it in the cargo area behind their seats, but the grandfather insisted he'd done this before with no problems.

Ian's desperation for money had won over common sense. Sure enough, twenty minutes into the flight, turbulence hit, and the lid popped off as the container shot out of the man's hands. Red juice had dumped all over the kid and plane.

"Dalll-ton."

The male voice bellowing interrupted Ian's internal rant. Straightening, he peered through the window of his Cessna's opened door to find Skip lumbering into the hangar. The forty-seven-year-old Inuit pilot had been the first person Ian met when he moved to Alaska from Virginia five months ago. Landing in Anchorage with no money, job, or place to live had been the second lowest point in his life. Skip had banged on the Cessna's door when Ian hadn't climbed out of the plane. Within a ten-minute conversation, Ian had a job prospect that ultimately gave him the other two missing needs: a paycheck and housing.

"What happened?" Skip crowded into Ian's space, studying the interior.

"Lack of judgment." Ian balled the wet T-shirt in his fist.

Skip cackled, straightening. "Yours or the passengers'?"

"Both." Ian threw the rag into the basket. He'd have cleaned the mess at the previous airport, but Skip had a tight schedule flying mail and packages to various villages. Skip only flew the items so far, so if the cargo had to reach the outer edges, he dropped it off at designated airports and other pilots hauled it the rest of the way. It wasn't a perfect system, but remote Alaskans were used to delays.

Brushing his long, graying braid over his shoulder, Skip's eyes twinkled. "I gotta charter for you."

"Seriously?" Ian perked up, maneuvering to look over Skip's shoulder. He caught the tail of the man's small white-and-gold Piper Chieftain, which revealed nothing.

"Come on." Skip stepped around the support bar securing the Cessna's wing overhead to the front of the plane. "We can catch her on the way to the lobby."

"Her?" Better and better. Then reality sunk in. Pretty, single women under the age of forty weren't that prevalent in the interior. In fact, they were downright scarce.

Skip's shoulders shook with his low laughter as he trundled toward the opening.

Whatever. Skip had a wife, four kids, and a grandchild. The man didn't have to bother with dating. Ian had almost had a wife, but his fiancée broke off their engagement not long before he moved to the wilds of Alaska. The breakup wasn't the reason for his new location, but it was a factor. At thirty-two, he thought he'd be settled by now, but five months ago, life had punched him in the face. With a sledgehammer.

Movement caught his attention and he hustled only to stop just inside the hangar.

Wha...? He blinked. Well, the potential passenger was under forty. She checked that box. Possibly pretty too, though the distance and her hat had the jury deliberating. Her single status remained a mystery, but that all paled with the flurry of questions now buzzing his brain.

Skip clapped Ian on the shoulder. "You said you needed more fares." He motioned. "I intercepted her in Anchorage. Gave her a free ride since I was coming here anyway."

Wind smacked Ian's cheeks, but he ignored the biting sting. What had happened to the poor woman?

A black sling held her right arm crooked at ninety degrees. So, either her arm, her shoulder, or both were broken. She winced as she walked, and her left hand rubbed the side of her ribs. Were they injured too? *Sheesh.* What drew a woman in that condition to the untamed Alaskan interior?

"Dog's a beauty, isn't she?"

Dog? Ian's gaze tracked lower, and sure enough, a gorgeous German shepherd stuck by the woman's side. More black than tan, the dog looked purebred and able to rip an arm off if warranted. No leash—

Wait.

"That's just wrong." The German shepherd didn't trot. "A dog that beautiful shouldn't be limping." Not that it was okay for *any* dog to be hurt, but something about watching *this* dog struggling made him want to lash out at whatever had caused the damage.

A deep sigh rumbled from the other pilot. "Agreed."

Ian plucked off his frayed baseball cap and scratched his scalp. His hair seriously needed a cut, but that was low on the list. "You know what happened to them?"

"Nah." Skip tucked his hands into his jeans. "Ms. Greene was quiet on the flight." He grinned. "I ended up doing most of the talking."

Ian snorted. That meant Skip told the woman his entire life story.

The older pilot's ears pinked. "Pictures might have been involved."

Laughter erupted out of Ian's throat. "No doubt."

Skip shoved Ian lightly. "Come on."

Slapping the hat back on, he followed Skip back into the hangar. In the last five months, the older pilot had drummed up, stumbled upon, and/or strong-armed countless charters for Ian. How the man did it, Ian didn't care. He desperately needed the money. The slew of attorneys back in Richmond drained their retainer fees almost as fast as Ian could replace them. Since he didn't see an end in sight, he pretty much accepted any legal charter.

And too many times to count, Ian wished he could afford to be picky. More than once, he regretted accepting a charter—the berry juice fiasco being one of them.

Skip peered over his shoulder and smiled. "This'll be the easiest money you make."

Chapter Two

Burnt coffee and stale popcorn invaded Natasha's nose the second she opened the glass door. It drowned every scent in the lobby.

A young girl, approximately fifteen or sixteen, sat behind a wood-paneled reception desk spanning at least ten feet. The top of a twenty-four-inch monitor peeked above the brown laminate overlay. The girl banged on an old keyboard while listening to someone on the multiline phone. Stacks of papers, a CB radio, mugs of pens and highlighters, and well-thumbed manuals left no room to utilize the desk. A giant map of Alaska was tacked to the wood-paneled wall behind her as well as some federally mandated signs.

The waiting area consisted of slouched couches in an L-shape. Three stalwart chairs had stains and tears, and a single side table held a leafy plant she couldn't identify, in surprisingly vibrant condition.

Closed doors on either side of the reception desk had no markings designating their purpose. Though, one of them had to lead to a kitchenette, based on the overpowering smell permeating the place.

The phone clattered back into the base, jolting Natasha's

gaze to the girl. Lexi leaned against Natasha's good leg to offer comfort.

"I'm Kaya," the teenager announced in a mix of boredom and curiosity. "Can I help you?"

"I, um—"

The door on the right side of the desk swung open, its hinges squeaking in protest.

The girl's head snapped in that direction, then her cheeks bloomed red as a goofy smile quirked her lips. "Ian." She stood so fast her rolling chair smacked into the wall. "I didn't see your plane land."

That statement revealed so much.

Two men, approximately the same height, five-ten-ish, crossed the threshold, allowing the door to slam shut on its own.

On reflex, Natasha cataloged the newcomers.

Skip, in his late forties, early fifties, smiled at Kaya. His weathered, indigenous face showed laugh lines and a life well lived. Braided hair reaching just shy of his waist had more white than black, and it looked good on him. Overall, he exuded peace and contentment.

Ian radiated curiosity, energy, and a vibe that didn't invite anyone to dig below the surface. Which made her instantly want to do just that. Ian looked to be in his early thirties. He wore a black T-shirt beneath a tan Carhartt jacket, and a pair of jeans gathered at the top of muddy steel-toed boots. A battered off-color baseball cap bearing a faded logo attempted to conceal dark brown hair, but the guy had let his locks grow or neglected regular haircuts. A full beard covered part of his cheeks and jaw, but he kept it shaved close. Light green eyes—a shade she'd never seen before—zeroed in on her. And stuck.

Unable to free herself from the gaze, she understood and respected the teenager's crush. Her own cheeks warmed under his intensity. But something deeper…a connection she didn't understand…hooked her. In all her twenty-eight years, she'd only felt this link one other time. When she met Lexi. The German shepherd was more than her partner—

"Ms. Greene."

Natasha forced her unwilling eyes to peer at Skip.

He swished his hands in presentation. "I'd like you to meet the pilot I told you about. Ian Dalton."

Natasha rolled the name in her mind and did her best to bite back the slew of questions fighting to break free. Why did he captivate her *and* look familiar? Had she seen him before? What was his story? She wanted answers to break this intrigue so she could focus on the reason for her trip.

The silence grew and she realized she hadn't said anything. "Hello."

Not a blink, twitch, or any indication the other pilot heard Skip's introduction or her response.

"Dalton." Skip's eyebrows drew down. "This is Natasha Greene and Lexi."

Lexi's head tilted at her name, but she didn't move from her position against Natasha's leg.

For too many heartbeats, nothing happened. Ian or Dalton or whatever he called himself continued to stare. Pale green eyes roved over her features, pausing on her tritoned baseball cap advertising a popular restaurant chain.

The blush crept down her neck, but she lifted her chin. Having only one free hand limited her options on maintaining midlength hair. Did he have a problem with her hat or was he gearing up to interrogate her about her injuries? For the past week, since she had been released from the hospital, she'd encountered two main reactions: one, people ignored the sling supporting a fractured collarbone and cast around a broken humerus, and all of her bruises, pretending they didn't exist, or two, people openly goggled and asked for the reason.

Ian Dalton obviously fell into the second category. She braced for the onslaught of questions that were none of his business.

Skip smacked the guy's shoulder. "Dalton."

Ian blinked out of the trance. What had just happened? One second, he walked through the door, the next he fell into a vortex.

"Don't be rude," Skip hissed next to Ian's ear.

Rude? What? He blinked again.

A low whine and the click of nails on concrete didn't make sense until his focus cleared. The gorgeous dog positioned itself to stand in front of its owner. Pointed ears and big eyes aimed at him in expectation.

Attempting to scratch his forehead, Ian's knuckles knocked his hat off-center.

"Yes, *Dalton*. Don't be rude."

Ian's gaze snapped to the beautiful woman five feet in front of him. Chapped lips flattened and traces of anger mottled with the colorful bruising marring her face. Dark hazel irises challenged him to explain himself. Only he couldn't. Never in his life had he fallen into a person's aura. Something about her made him want to run away as far and as fast as he could. His gut yelled that if he didn't turn around right now, she'd change his life forever.

That made no sense. Pushing the dubious feelings aside, he fixed his hat. "Sorry." His cheeks heated. Did he try to explain the reason for his staring, not that he understood it himself? Nope. He'd only dig himself into a hole. "Miss…" *Oh no*. The heat flamed higher on his skin. "I, uh, didn't catch your name."

A single brown eyebrow lifted.

"Dalton," Skip groaned, clapping a hand over his face.

Yeah, yeah. "Ian Dalton." He thrust his right hand forward to shake— "Oh. Um." He dropped his arm, eyeing the sling. *Oaf.* His brain had disconnected along with his manners. Hopefully both would be back online soon.

"Natasha Greene." She motioned with her free hand toward the dog. "And this is Lexi."

Lexi seemed to smirk at him.

As far as first impressions went, he'd rate himself a solid one out of ten. *Great job.*

"If you're looking for a pilot," Kaya chirped, leaning against the reception desk, "Ian's the *best.*"

Dalton inwardly cringed at the dreamy declaration. He didn't know how to handle the teenager's crush. He kept ignoring it, hoping Kaya would get the hint, but so far it hadn't worked.

"Is he?" Natasha asked. One eyebrow lifted again.

That stung. His ego apparently remained healthy.

"Oh, for sure." Kaya either didn't pick up on the doubt or ignored it.

"Hey," Skip protested, resting his hands on his hips. "What about me?"

The airport phone began ringing.

"Uncle Skip." Kaya whirled to answer the call.

"You two talk over there." Skip motioned to the empty waiting area. "I'm going to eat lunch. I've got to get back in the air."

"Sorry, Skip." Ian didn't know why he apologized. The older pilot brought him the fare; Ian hadn't baled on lunch.

"Nothing to be sorry for." The hinges squealed at Skip opening the door. "I've got some priority packages today, so I can't linger." Without waiting for a response, he crossed the threshold to the restricted area and the door smacked shut behind him.

Right. Okay. Now to put a bandage on the bleeding wound he'd caused to his reputation. Striding to the depressing lounge—Whisper *really* needed to replace the outdated and worn furniture—Ian steeled himself to grovel. He couldn't afford to alienate a potential customer.

"Mr. Dalton—"

"Just Dalton's fine." He settled his weight over his feet and his mind blanked. He had no clue how to start repairing the mess he'd made of the introductions.

"Okay. Dalton," Natasha repeated, her lyrical voice stiff. "I'm trying to find someone. Skip told me you specialize in flying passengers."

"I've hauled cargo." His pride, once again, reared its head. *Grovel, Ian.* "But, yeah, most of my flights have been passengers." He'd prefer a steady cargo route like Skip's, but he'd quickly grown a reputation among the other bush pilots. His willingness to execute dangerous off-airport landings had netted him a lot of hunters, scientists, and nature enthusiasts.

Natasha exhaled. "Great. Have you had any solo travelers lately? I'm looking for a man."

Ian could take that announcement multiple ways, until his gaze dropped to her injuries. "This guy responsible for all that?" The question popped out before he could hold it back.

Fury flashed in her expression and Lexi stiffened. A low growl rumbled from the dog's throat.

Ian froze. This conversation was going downhill fast. Normally he had an easygoing charm with people, but this woman robbed him of the natural ability. Maybe he deserved the dog's wicked teeth sinking into his hide.

"It's okay, girl," Natasha whispered, her left hand stroking the black-and-tan fur. The dog relaxed and nudged her snout against the woman's stomach. Natasha lifted her gaze from the German shepherd to meet Ian's. "We've been together for four years. She senses my moods and interprets my body language, then responds accordingly."

"She going to bite me if you get mad?" His attempt at humor felt stiff and flat.

"Only if I give her the command." Natasha's lips quirked. "Or if I'm unconscious and she thinks you're a threat. Then she'll attack."

"Good to know." He swallowed, doing his best to radiate harmless vibes. "The man you're searching for, did he give you those injuries?" For some reason, he couldn't let the topic go.

"Yes."

He rocked back onto his heels at the blunt response. "And you're going after him? By yourself?" *Have you lost your mind?* He had enough sense to hold that last question back.

She blew out a breath and peered at the sliver of scenery showing through the grimy front door.

Thick, straight brown hair, almost the same as his dark shade, straddled her shoulder. The locks had been pulled through the sizing hole in the back of the cap. Small silver studs adorned her ears and no makeup painted her face. Not that she needed it. Once the bruises healed, she'd have flawless tanned skin. The lightweight, zip-up jacket in shades of charcoal and black concealed the reason her right arm needed a sling, but he imagined she had at least one cast.

"It's complicated," she finally answered, turning her attention back to him. "I'm not going to confront the man, I just have to find his location. That's where you come in. I don't care how many flights it takes, or how many days this stretches, as long as we unearth his position."

His meager bank account cried "Hallelujah." A small part of him secretly hoped it took many, *many* flights.

Lexi limped into the space between Ian and Natasha. This mystery man had hurt a dog. A. Dog. And a woman.

Those facts offended his moral code and he wished he could help Natasha for free.

"Have you flown a man by himself lately?" She seemed to hold her breath.

"Yep." He nodded a little too enthusiastically. This woman had him too rattled. "I've had a few solo flights. One a few days ago."

Dark hazel irises lightened as a smile drew her lips upward. "I've got cash."

Those three beautiful words sealed the deal.

Chapter Three

Natasha tried not to squirm, but the bulky lap belt strapped over her upper thighs dug in too hard. Once they reached altitude, she'd loosen the dark gray polyester. Hopefully her legs wouldn't be asleep from blood loss by then.

Settled in the left copilot seat, she did her best not to touch anything. Dials, switches, and levers were all within reach. The two-grip yoke in front of her twisted and slid in and out with every adjustment Dalton made, sometimes scraping her legs. She could just imagine inadvertently bumping something, causing them to crash. None of the seating in the cramped plane had any separation or armrests, so every time he moved, he ground against her bruised ribs and broken humerus and jostled her fractured collarbone. He moved constantly.

Sweat popped beneath her hat, and her teeth hurt from clenching her jaw. With her left side already against the frame, she had nowhere to go, no room to maneuver, no way to stop the pain. The cherry on top of her misery sundae was the two rudder pedals hogging valuable floor space. She had to jam her combat boots against the underside of the seat.

Lord, please help me survive this. She exhaled slowly. Since the old plane had no harnesses for dogs, Dalton had rigged two cargo nets to the ceiling and floor—one right behind their row, the second behind two cloth/leather seats. Lexi sprawled across the cushions within, staring out the small window on the left side. In the area at the very back, Dalton had shoved her two pieces of luggage and his gear.

"It smells like a juice farm had a party in here," she stated into the microphone centimeters from her mouth, which connected to oversize headphones over her ears.

Dalton flinched, his fists tightening on the grips. "Don't ask."

Okay, then. At least the overwhelming berry scent replaced the remnants of obnoxious coffee and popcorn clinging to her jacket.

Thick white clouds had moved in, stealing the tiny bit of warmth from the sun. She should've added a sweater to her layers before they took off, but she'd been too eager to start the search. Besides, the less he knew about the extent of her injuries, the better.

Nope. Stop. Thinking about her bruised, broken, and fractured bones only made them throb harder, which, then, led to her recalling the reason she was on medical leave.

The Cessna leveled.

Whoa. Her complaints faded away.

What. A. View. Indescribable beauty spread as far as the eye could see. Towering mountains in shades of slate, white, and brown sprawled. Miles of full, green trees rose to immense heights, carpeting jagged and rolling terrain. Tributaries and rivers snaked, hiding their final destinations.

A majestic spectacle untouched by man. TV shows and documentaries paled against the amazing pageantry and vastness. Gorgeous and terrifying. As a city girl born and raised, her comfort zone included tall buildings, aggressive traffic, and lots of pedestrians. Sure, she'd vacationed in rural and scenic destinations, but this…imposing, *forbidding* landscape was a whole new level.

Dalton's elbow knocked into her arm cast. She slapped her gaping mouth closed, gritting her teeth against the fresh round of pain.

"Woof."

Natasha peered through the gap in the seats to find the German shepherd shoving her snout between the yellow gridding.

"It's okay." She uttered that line way too often lately. Nothing about this was okay, and the dog knew it. But they had to forge ahead.

Needing distance from her thoughts, she focused on her new companion. The intriguing man gave off a myriad of conflicting vibes. On the surface, he appeared charming, though their first conversation hadn't showcased that *at all*. Only her honed experience and years of reading people told her he usually lured with easy smiles. But charmers beguiled as a way to keep people at a distance. They didn't invite anyone to go below the surface, and Dalton radiated that he only wanted to pilot, not chitchat or become friends. Too bad.

He had no problem taking her money nor did he balk at draining her bank account with more flights. The average person would've pressed for a modicum of details, but not him. Not a single additional question. Odd, when she thought for sure he fit into the second category of people who stared and demanded answers for her injuries.

The contradictions tempted her love of solving mysteries. As a K-9 officer with the Philadelphia Police Department, she made her living off hunting for answers. And her instincts warned that Ian Dalton didn't add up. She might've let it go if he hadn't touched something deep inside her. Only Lexi had grabbed her soul at first sight. Chills rippled over Natasha's skin. Why had this pilot trig-

gered the same reaction? She didn't want or need this complication. She'd flown across the country for *one* reason
and stumbling into a potential life partner wasn't it. At all.
Pretty much the opposite of her mission.

Maybe she'd misread their first meeting. Yeah. She
grabbed on to the thought and held it tight. God knew her
reasons for finding Randy Puckett were imperative. He
wouldn't dilute her purpose by throwing a soulmate at
her now. It didn't make sense. Therefore, she misjudged
Dalton's importance. Besides, her soulmate wouldn't be a
walking inconsistency that made her believe he hid something. Her life partner would be open, honest, and trust-
worthy.

Exhaling with relief, she decided to assuage her curiosity to pass the time. Starting with the nagging feeling
she'd seen Dalton before. "You look familiar."

Since The Incident that landed her in the hospital, she'd
been stuck at home watching TV. Too much TV. Adding
news programs and educational documentaries didn't combat the mindless bingeing.

Color leached from Dalton's cheeks.

Her curiosity deepened. "We haven't met before," she
mused aloud. "But I'm almost positive I've seen your face."
Maybe he'd been featured in a newsclip about bush flying.

Dalton cleared his throat. "We're coming up on the
Yukon River."

Natasha snapped her gaze to the side window. Sure
enough, the wide body of water cut through the forest.
Still as a peaceful lake. She expected rapids or churning
restlessness. Maybe that existed in other sections.

Turning away, she studied Dalton again. He had de-
flected her statement like a pro. That only made her want
to dig deeper. "How long have you been a bush pilot?"

Sunglasses covered his eyes, but she could tell he shifted
his attention between the dials and the sky beyond. "I've

been flying my whole life, thanks to my uncle." His tinny voice bounced in her headphones. "Got my pilot's license before my driver's license."

"Here, in Alaska?" With no roads in most of the state, she imagined a lot of residents learned to fly.

Dalton's grip on the yoke tightened.

She narrowed her eyes at his lack of response. "Where are you from?"

The skin on his fists whitened. "Richmond."

Virginia. Not what she expected, but why the reluctance to answer?

"That's a long way from Whisper, Alaska." She didn't need to know anything about his background. He had a right to privacy and didn't have to tell her anything. She could back off, but his reactions weren't normal. Weren't consistent with a reclusive person. They were more in line with someone who had something to hide. "Why the change?"

"I bought the Cessna from my uncle." He patted the dented and scarred instrument panel. "This baby is fifty-four years old and still going strong."

It looked every one of those years. Scratched, red wings topped the plane and the white-and-blue body needed a fresh coat of paint. Two larger wheels in the front and a smaller wheel at the tail had the Cessna naturally resting at an angle on the ground.

"I needed a change, so I decided to try my hand at bush piloting," he continued. "It's not for the faint of heart. Most of my charters are off-airport."

Off. Airport. "What's that mean?" Trepidation slinked down her spine.

"Pretty much what you think. No runways. No designated landing places." His gaze shifted to his side window, then back. "I have to find relatively flat spots that are long enough, and pray it works out."

"You're kidding." Heart slamming into her chest, she gripped her thigh with her left hand.

He chuckled, though it contained no mirth. "Look out the window. Do you think airports exist out here? They don't. Only where the area's been settled. Alaskans are vigilant about preserving nature. They leave land how they found it. Those teachings are passed down from generation to generation."

Embarrassment flushed her skin. She had assumed Alaska was similar to the rest of the United States: airports scattered throughout, with pockets of preserved/protected land. *Foolish.* Her focus had been on finding Randy Puckett, the bomb maker responsible for her injuries and so many casualties, not studying the geography. Her ignorance tasted like ash on her tongue.

In her mind, her plan had been easy. Hop on a plane, ferret out the criminal, then call in law enforcement for an arrest. So naive. And she hadn't been naive in a long, long time.

"What reason did the solo flight give you last week?" She had to learn everything she could. Develop a better strategy. Do something other than eat humble pie.

"Hunting." Dalton glanced at her, a frown tugging at his mouth. "You okay? You're looking kinda green. Need a puke bag?"

"I'm fine," she snapped, hating that she showed weakness.

"Woof, woof. Growwwwwl."

"Lexi." Natasha adjusted her tone. "Quiet."

Silence reigned in the cabin, outside the noisy engine. The dog pushed her snout through the netting again while Dalton focused on flying.

"Hunting," she repeated to resume her initial questioning. "Did he have the usual gear?"

Dalton shrugged. "Had all kinds of packs." He scratched

his beard. "Different shapes and sizes. More than I've seen before, but who am I to know what a guy needs when he's surviving weeks by himself."

"Weeks?" Natasha's pulse quickened. "He told you he'd be in the wilderness for that long?" This could mean a timeline might already be in play for the next bombing. "Did he set a time for pickup?"

Dalton shook his head.

Natasha deflated.

"I just figured it'd be that long, since most hunters go out for extended periods of time." He glanced at her again. "It takes a while to track big game like caribou and bears—"

"When you landed, did you see anyone else?" Was she chasing the bomb maker or an avid gamesman looking for peace by blasting holes in the wildlife?

"Nope."

The plane shook violently just as a warning tone blared in the cabin.

What did that signal mean?

"Hold on," Dalton shouted.

Natasha grabbed the strap mounted above the side window.

Wrestling with the yoke, Dalton tried to counter the bobbing and dipping.

Wishing for the puke bag now, Natasha frantically searched for the cause.

"Turbulence." Strain oozed from every part of Dalton.

The view beyond the windows disappeared. Nothing but white and gray surrounded them. Clouds. From the ground, they appeared harmless. Now she feared their existence.

"Can you go below them?" she shouted.

"I don't know what's below us." Dalton fought the yoke.

Oh, Lord, help us. Why hadn't she paid better attention to their surroundings?

"Air traffic control?" she tried again to be helpful.

"Doesn't exist out here."

Of course it didn't.

Eternity stretched as Dalton dueled with the air currents battering the Cessna. The random dipping, jerking, and sliding cured her of enjoying amusement parks for life.

The warning tone ceased.

The convulsing steadied, the current occasionally buffeting the plane.

They broke free of the cloud and the vista, once again, spread below.

"I think I just lost five years of my life." Her body trembled and she had trouble forcing her hand to let go of the strap.

"Welcome to bush flying." Dalton settled into his seat.

She had the overwhelming urge to smack him, laugh maniacally, or do both.

"We're headed toward the Nowitna National Wildlife Refuge." He craned his neck to see out the front and side windows, then checked a dial showing coordinates. "Correction. We're already there. Means we have to circle back. We're too far south."

No. She couldn't handle any more turbulence. "Can we skip the clouds and carnival ride?" The wobble in her voice was totally understandable.

"Absolutely." He pushed on the yoke. "The lower altitude should have smoother air."

Thankfully nothing hampered their ability to remain below the chaos.

"I keep a log of coordinates—" Dalton kept checking the panel "—where I pick up and drop off passengers."

Hallelujah. That made searching for the bomb maker easier. *If* the man had chartered with Dalton. She'd deal with that ominous thought later. For now, she kept quiet. Dalton seemed to be searching for something.

She peered through the side glass, not sure what he

sought. Rows and rows of evergreen trees blanketed the land, their tops swaying in the wind. Intermittent openings revealed large swaths of green-and-yellow vegetation. Some clearings had small streams cutting through and disappearing into the forest. Ahead emerged steep hills covered in more green and yellow, stretching for a mile circumference. Within the valley of the two hills, a watery sandbar cut a path.

Dalton muttered something she didn't catch.

"What's wrong?" Her heart climbed her throat. Were they lost? Had the turbulence done something awful to the plane?

"Rains hit this area hard." The Cessna banked to the right. Gravity forced her to fall against him.

White noise overwhelmed her senses as her jostled broken/fractured bones stole her ability to think.

She shuddered, the tips of her left fingers smacking the window in an attempt to find the strap—

The plane leveled, helping her sit straight.

Lord, help me. Air sawed through her mouth until she bit her lip to keep from crying.

"...last time I was here..."

She tried to concentrate on Dalton's voice, using it to master the pain.

"...dry, but now..."

Come on. You can do this. Natasha squeezed her eyes shut and exhaled.

"Can't be helped."

What couldn't be helped? Her eyelids popped open.

Only then did she realize the plane was descending, aiming for the crevasse between the steep hills. Rushing water formed a stream that split and came together. The closer they descended, the more she realized jagged pebbles and rocks covered the land.

No. He wouldn't, *couldn't* land here.

"Terrain," a computerized female voice blared. *"Pull up. Pull up."*

"Brace yourself," Dalton barked, as his fists clamped the yoke.

Lord God, help. She'd barely thought the prayer when the plane's front wheels smacked down, rattling her brain.

The aircraft jolted, bobbing into the air to smack down again. Water whooshed. The Cessna jostled left and right.

Branches from sporadic evergreen trees reached for the wings, their needles brushing the red paint.

Dalton struggled to control the landing, his mouth a flat line.

The front wheels rammed into something hard. A horrendous screeching hurt her ears as the Cessna lurched.

"No!" Dalton yelled.

The screeching stopped, but the plane didn't. It shuddered, smacking against the terrain, threatening to overturn. Without warning, it veered left.

A towering evergreen grew larger in the front windshield.

No—

The plane slammed into the unforgiving tree, throwing her forward...

Chapter Four

"*Ruff. Ruff. Ruff.*"

Ian twitched. The peaceful darkness faded with the invasion of the annoying noise.

"*Grrrrrr. Ruff. Ruff. Ruff.*"

What is *that?* Nothing made sense.

"*Wooof. Wooof. Hoowwwwlll.*"

He jolted awake.

Glorious ignorance vanished, and his ribs wailed in agony. Something wet tickled his cheek as his forehead throbbed like a pulse.

Good news? The airbag in the lap belt had deployed. No catapulting through the front windshield for him. Yay.

Bad news? He must have been out for longer than a minute. The airbag had fully deflated. His body had then tried to become one with the instrument panel.

"*Ruff. Ruff. Ruff. Grrrrrr.*"

"I'm awake." The words slurred together and he grimaced at the wet, coppery taste landing on his tongue.

The barking stopped.

"I don't want to be," he muttered, the statement barely intelligible.

Cracking his eyelids, he winced at the light drilling into his aching head. Daylight lasted about sixteen hours this time of year and decided to make its presence known by piercing his skull.

Groaning, he slapped his lids closed and mentally surveyed his body. Fingers and toes wiggled. No paralysis. Excellent news. That was the extent of his medical knowledge. He probably had a concussion and maybe bruised or fractured ribs. He wouldn't know until he—

His eyelids popped open. "Barking. Dog."

As if on cue, a protracted whine filtered through Ian's muzzy brain.

"Dog." Awareness cleaved the fog. "Lexi." The name was out before he consciously remembered it.

Another thought barreled in. "Natasha." *Passenger.*

Like a bolt of lightning, adrenaline shot through his veins. Slapping his hands against the broken panel, he pushed. Plastic creaked and pieces fell.

He *hurt*! If he had any faith left, he'd beg the Lord for help. But he didn't, so he relied on the adrenaline to see him through.

"Natasha." The more he turned his head, the more his vision blurred and stars began to dance. His neck screamed for him to stop, but he kept going. He had to see, to know if she survived.

Lexi whined.

Ian blinked a few times, finding the dog's snout shoved through the cargo netting, which had somehow remained in place. His rigging had worked. The ceiling and floor clips held against the tremendous force. How many injuries Lexi sustained still remained a mystery though.

Snapping his attention to his other passenger, he choked on an inhale. *Oh, Lord...* This time, he had no problem praying. Ian just hoped God paid attention. "Natasha."

The woman lay unmoving, curled over the instrument panel, similar to his former position.

His trembling hand grasped her bicep. Something hard... His fingers explored. A cast prevented him from squeezing. Was that the reason for the sling or did she have more injuries to her arm or shoulder?

Not important. Did she have a pulse?

The lap belt airbag had protected her upper body when it thrust forward. Blood dripped from various cuts on her face. How much more damage did this woman have to survive?

"Hey." He prodded her cast. *Bad idea. Broken bone inside.* His palm slid up to her shoulder and found it thick, as if wrapped by something. *Ace bandage?* Shoulder injury and broken upper arm explained the sling. What *else* was on the list before she climbed into his plane?

"Natasha," he called again, pouring more energy into his voice. His adrenaline waned, his own injuries gobbling the initial rush. "Hey. Wake up."

A constant dull ringing added to the confusion in his brain.

"*Please* don't be dead." He could *not* bear her death on his conscience. Not only that, the investigators back in Richmond would just *love* to add his causing her demise to their list of accusations against him. A multi-jurisdictional task force was convinced he was a prime player in a scheme that transported illegal merchandise within legitimate cargo. And they hadn't been discreet about their smuggling allegations either. Thanks to them, Dalton had lost his job and fiancée.

"*Woof. Woof. Woof.*" Growling low, Lexi surged forward, then jerked her head to the right. "*Woof. Woof. Woof.*"

The tenor of the bark had changed. Never owning an animal, Ian didn't speak dog or understand the meanings of the different tones, but his muddled brain translated this message: *look outside, human.*

"Wake up!"

Something jabbed Natasha's side.

Darkness cradled her brain, sucking her deeper into the void—

"Woof. Woof. Woof. Groooowl. Woof. Woof. Woof."

Lexi. *Something's wrong.* The dog only barked like that when she was distressed or sensed a threat.

"Natasha," a deep male voice commanded, then another jab in the side. "Wake up."

Wake up? Had she fallen asleep? Nothing made sense.

Consciousness rose, forcing the darkness to recede. Bit by bit, she recalled her journey across the country. Why?

Bomb maker.

Awareness flooded, bringing with it pain. *Lord, help.*

"Come on…"

She snapped her eyes open at the insistent male voice. Comprehension of his words escaped her, but he kept yelling anyway.

Who? The masculine face only inches from hers had a trimmed beard coated with blood on the one side. Why did he—

Plane crash. "Lexi," she wheezed.

"Ruff. Ruff. Ruff."

"Natasha." The man's breath puffed against her skin. "Can you hear me?"

"Yeah." A parched throat prevented her from speaking easily. "Lexi," she said again, needing to know her partner was okay.

"She's fine." Ian…no…Dalton narrowed his eyes. "Can you move?"

Probably. Did she want to? Not. At. All.

"Company's coming."

Was he speaking a new form of English? She understood the words individually, but together, they didn't make sense. Then clarity dawned.

"Company?" Her gaze tried to see around him, but the little glimpse showed a steep hill through the broken glass.

"You understand me." He sighed, and the sound was rattled and painful. "You're going to be fine. No brain damage."

Ignoring his rambling about her medical status, her

mind leaped into processing scenarios. *Company* could mean anything. Hunters on their way to help after hearing the crash. *Or.* The bomb maker and his cronies coming to investigate, then eliminate the threat. I.e., the three of them.

"How many?" Adrenaline hurtled through her bloodstream. "Do they have weapons?"

Dalton stopped yammering and gaped.

"Come on." She didn't wait for an answer. "We have to move." She lifted her left arm, groaning at the stabbing radiating from her fractured ribs. White lights danced in her vision.

"Move?" Ian repeated. "You shouldn't do anything." He sucked in air through his teeth as he shifted to face forward. "Let me see if they can help—"

"*No*," Natasha barked, frustrated she couldn't grab his arm to stop him. Sharp edges dug into her left palm as she pushed herself off the infernal yoke. The grips did their best to break the rest of her right arm.

What was all this material? Yards of dull white nylon covered her legs. Airbag. From the lap belt. *Thank You, Lord.*

"You're not thinking clearly." Dalton began to shift toward his broken window.

"Stop."

He froze at her command.

"Until we know if they're friendly or not—"

"This is Alaska," he cut in, his brows lowered. "Not a war zone—"

"We don't have time for this." She swayed, blinking back the sleepiness trying to drag her under. If the fog would just let go of her brain and let her *think* properly. "Trust me, okay?"

"Why?" Ian challenged. "What aren't you telling me?"

Her pounding head ruled the chaos in her mind. Why

had she wanted to hide her real purpose for traveling to Alaska? Her reason must have been solid, but no answer revealed itself. Truth won. "I'm a K-9 officer with the Philadelphia police." Nausea climbed her throat. "Lexi is my partner." She swallowed the lump back. "We were injured chasing a bomb maker. The very man who might be headed toward us now."

Ian blinked once. Twice. Three times. "Are you kidding me?"

"Still want to see if the 'company' is friendly?"

He snapped his mouth closed.

"Out of the plane. Now."

Chapter Five

Standing outside the Cessna, Ian snatched at the clip securing the cargo netting to the floor. Twice he missed unclasping the metal. His fury and concussion hampered his ability to focus.

"Dalton, hurry up."

He almost whirled but managed to stay put. Looking at the deceitful woman now would only ratchet up his blood pressure, which almost had him coding.

A black-and-tan face wiggled into the sliver between the netting and open door frame. Lexi pushed against Ian's aching ribs in her bid for freedom.

The clasp finally sprang open.

Ian had barely stepped back when the German shepherd launched out of the smashed Cessna.

Bugs had quieted, birds were scarce, and no animals ventured into sight. Male voices drifted toward him in the eerie silence. Snatches of conversation from the four men trekking down the steep hill on the other side of the ravine were garbled. He couldn't understand a single word.

Paranoia insidiously took hold. Who were those men carrying assault rifles? No one hunted animals with automatic firepower.

Pivoting to face the woman examining the dog, he hissed, "How could you lie to me?"

"I don't think she broke anything," Natasha mused. "She's moving—"

"Don't ignore me." Ian marched toward the pair, every step jostling his ribs and pounding head.

Natasha scanned the steep hill on their side.

The once-glorious Cessna hid the three of them from the approaching group's view.

"We'll fight later," she uttered in a low voice, then made a specific motion with her right hand dangling from the sling. Lexi's ears pricked and she silently maneuvered to Natasha's left side. "We need to find a place to hide."

If his blood wasn't already thrumming, he'd swear a vein burst. Nothing about this was right or okay.

Following Natasha and Lexi, Ian grimaced, tucking behind a towering black spruce. The same black spruce that had smashed his plane. His prized possession and only source of income. Thanks to the ominous investigation in Richmond, he doubted his insurance company would expedite his claim. He'd be amazed if they reviewed it in the next three months. What did insurance adjustors care about pesky things like rent, food, and bottomless attorney retainers?

If he didn't throw up from the concussion, that realization might trigger it.

Natasha leaned close, her sling brushing his zippered jacket. "It's not ideal," she whispered, "but we should split up. Use the boulders, trees, and plants—" she pointed to the obstacles "—to hide as we climb the hill."

"You think they won't figure it out and follow us?" The question pushed through clenched teeth.

"Yes." A frown creased her brows. "But it's the best we can do at the moment."

Too many words crowded his mouth, each trying to fly through first.

"Lexi, scout." Natasha signed with her left hand, then pointed to the large dirty boulder fifty feet up and to the left, jutting among the knee-to-waist-to-six-feet-tall vegetation.

Blueberry and bearberry bushes covered the hill, their blue-and-red fruit in abundance. Tall thickets of Scouler's and Bebb's willow shrubs flourished, their twigs bursting with leaves, and weeds of all types filled in the gaps.

The dog's belly hit the ground and she became camouflaged among it all.

Lexi tried to slink forward but quivered instead. She whined, cranking her neck to peer up at Natasha.

The sad sight stabbed Ian's heart, dulling the fury.

"Release." Natasha's command quavered. "It's okay."

Lexi's legs trembled as she stood.

The men's shouts grew louder. They were closing in.

"Aim for the boulder," Natasha flung at Ian as she made another hand sign at Lexi. "Try to blend in."

He was not James Bond. Before he moved to Alaska, he'd worked construction full time. No skulking or sneaking required.

The thought of a bomb maker headed his way spurred him to clamp his mouth closed and lower into a crouch. It *hurt*. His ribs did *not* want any part of hunching, and his bruised brain seconded the complaint. Still, he forced himself to utilize the tall willow shrubs as much as possible to wend a path toward the boulder.

Natasha's infuriating injuries prevented her from skulking like Dalton and vanishing in the vegetation like Lexi.

Less complaining, more moving.

If by moving, her command meant stumble and almost fall every few seconds, she was breaking world records.

Blue-and-red berries burst against her black tactical pants. A sneeze threatened to release. Her body was reacting to something; plants, fresh air, human-eating animals roaming the area… It didn't help the abundance of flora had *strong* competing aromas.

She puffed, gritting her teeth at the incline working against her. Lexi remained close, her long tongue hanging out the side of her opened mouth as she limped, using three legs, sometimes the fourth, to navigate the harrowing growth.

Did snakes live this far north? That unwelcome question popped into Natasha's head and she almost tripped. She *hated* snakes. And bugs of all kinds. Chills rippled over her skin and she had to stop from kicking the vegetation to pummel anything that might be slithering near.

Masculine hails from behind had her dashing around a six-foot-tall bush wide enough to hide three people. The myriad of twigs with intense green leaves promised to snag her clothing. Nature had more pitfalls and danger than the city.

Peering to the right, she silently groaned. She should already be at the boulder. At this rate, the men would find her in minutes.

At least four distinct voices argued. All in Russian.

Her street informant back in Philly had been right.

These men were no friendly hunters. Her stomach plunged at her latest circumstances. The plane crash put her at a major disadvantage. A probable concussion added to her liability list was *not* ideal.

Play the cards you're dealt, her grandfather loved to preach.

According to her informant, rumors circulated that the bomb maker who set off the explosion near the Liberty Bell where she and Lexi had been injured had struck a deal with the Russian Mafia and was meeting the criminal organization in northwestern Alaska.

She had passed the information to her lieutenant, but he ultimately dismissed the lead.

Yet, here was a group of armed Russians headed her way. She had to let the lieutenant know. Slapping her right coat pocket, she felt for the bulky satellite phone—

No. She futilely—awkwardly—jammed her left fingers inside. *Gone.* Her lifeline must have fallen out in the crash.

Another spate of Russian jolted her into action.

Against her training and instincts, she turned her back on the potential threat and continued plodding up the slope. She was only supposed to do reconnaissance. Fly to potential locations, take her time scouting with Lexi's help, then call in law enforcement once she had confirmation.

Nowhere in her plan did she expect to crash-land, add to her injuries, and attempt to flee in her condition. Her success rate decreased dramatically.

The shrink in her police-mandated weekly sessions had warned Natasha that her moods and rational thinking would be affected by the horrific trap she and Lexi had barely survived. Natasha had inwardly scoffed. Now she wished she'd listened to the woman.

Nothing had gone right since Dalton stepped into the airport lobby. Her unexpected connection to him started the skew to her plan and their wreck further deviated everything.

Sweat poured down Natasha's face, mixing with the blood still trickling from her forehead.

Surveying the hill for her next hiding place, she realized she'd never make it to the boulder. Too much space with knee-high plants had her in the open too long.

Frustration exhaled over dry lips. Walking straight up was the hardest. Climbing on an angle had been her goal.

Heavy wheezing rumbled from Lexi's chest. Neither of them had escaped the bomb maker's trap unscathed—

A strong grip encircled her left forearm. Snapping her gaze over, she found the furious face of Dalton inches from her own.

"You gotta move," he whisper-ordered. "They keep looking up this hill."

That meant they might decide to find the missing passengers. Which was them.

Chapter Six

Randy Puckett snatched the bulky satellite phone off the stained wooden surface. The annoying ringtone buzzed like an irritating fly, ruining his concentration. Clamping a hand on his sweaty neck, he soothed the agitated skin.

"What?" he barked, flinging his hand away from his neck.

"No one here." The thick Russian accent made the words almost indecipherable.

Gazing at the uneven boards on the low ceiling, Randy counted to five. He really didn't need another complication right now. "Did you look around the whole plane?"

The fact he felt the need to ask the simple question said a lot about his confidence in the combined brain power of the four men.

"*Da, da.* We search front, sides, back. Nothing."

Unease slithered down Randy's spine. He didn't care that the plane crashed. He wanted to know the reason it was in the area in the first place. The Russians had assured him this part of Alaska was isolated. No one for at least fifty miles. The Mafia had built this structure ages ago to blend in with the forest and no one had noticed.

But now a downed plane sat too close to the hideout. The crash had been loud and jarring, spurring them into high alert. Only a few trusted people on Randy's end knew of his location…

He straightened. Not true. He'd hired a bush pilot at the last minute. That man also knew Randy's general where-abouts. He cursed. He should've killed the man after they landed. At the time, he worried it would attract attention, but now he wondered if he had miscalculated.

Kicking an empty cardboard box, he blamed the Russians. They should've had a backup pilot on hand. The original had been severely injured by a bear while schlep-ping supplies to the hideout.

A small sprinkle of dirt cascaded from a crack in the ceiling slats. "Did you find anything—"

"Da," Pasha interrupted, a bad habit Randy despised. "Luggage and backpack."

That stopped Randy's pacing. Why would the pilot leave his luggage behind? Was he hurt and searching for help? More importantly, was Randy's operation in danger? Had the FBI or police hired the pilot to fly them to Randy's last known location?

His imagination spiraled as his pacing ate up the floor-ing.

"'ello?" Pasha asked, breaking through the escalating scenarios of failure.

His latest partnership with the Russians was the last step of years worth of planning and strategic offenses. He *had* to finish the bombs the Mafia contracted or they'd withhold payment. Instead of money, they were supply-ing explosives and equipment he desperately needed and couldn't buy in the United States. Randy's militia, no, the entire region of militias, counted on him to build a set of specialized devices to kick-start a civil war.

"'ello?" Pasha asked again.

Randy needed to think. To plan. "Have one of your men stay with the plane." He went to scrub his face, but caught sight of his filthy palm. "Send another to scout the area. If he doesn't find a trace of the pilot in the next hour, have him return. You and the last man strip the aircraft of everything useful and bring it back here." He hung up before Pasha could respond.

His heavy boots clomped over the wooden flooring, which was in desperate need of repair. He passed the doorway to his sanctuary on the way to the small kitchenette and paused just outside. Plastic sheeting enclosed the room with overlapping flaps at its entrance. The only truly clean space in the place.

Five six-foot tables groaned beneath the weight of sensitive equipment and parts as well as computers linked to a private satellite the government couldn't access.

Ideas began to formulate. Ways he could secure the hideout and establish a perimeter warning system. If his measures happened to go boom, all the better.

Ian, Natasha, and Lexi had crested the hill and slipped into the forest a little while ago, but he couldn't tell if they were safe. Had the men gone back to wherever they made camp? Or were they searching for the missing occupants? He had no clue and didn't risk stopping long enough to find out.

His limited knowledge of survival didn't stretch to evading a gun-toting bomb maker and his lethal buddies.

Natasha's skin grew paler. Sweat coated her face, making the blood dripping from her cuts seem garish.

Poor Lexi's tongue hung from the side of her mouth.

"We need to stop." Natasha's chapped lips were to the point of cracking.

Compassion dulled his anger. He wished he was a callous man. Someone who could leave her and her problems behind to save himself. But his father and uncle had raised him with a strong moral code.

Slowing their pace, he scanned the surroundings. Soaring black, white, and Sitka spruces dominated the land. Weeds competed with the myriad of underbrush, which did their best to find patches of sunlight in the canopy. Their many twigs reached high and wide, not offering an easy pathway through.

As it was, it took a lot of work to trudge through the thicket and he worried they left an obvious trail. If the men did try to find them, it wouldn't take long.

The .44 Magnum revolver secured to his waist, hidden by his jacket, weighed heavy. He kept it to use against wild animals. Never did he imagine aiming it at a person. *No.*

He shut that line of thinking down. He would *not* put himself in a position to take someone's life. *But you already did*, a small voice whispered in his mind. *You flew Natasha and her dog without knowing all the facts.* And now they were stranded.

Dread mingled with anger. If only he'd thought beyond the money.

"Dalton." Natasha pointed. "How 'bout there?"

Before he could zero in on what she indicated, Natasha made the same hand sign as earlier. "Lexi, scout."

Soft rustling in the shrubs on the left was the only indication he had of the dog's position.

As much as he wanted to demand answers from Natasha, he forced himself to wait a little longer. Once they were safe, he'd confront the woman. No more withholding information. She'd tell him everything.

Another bout of paranoia attacked. She'd alluded to recognizing him. Had she already known about the federal task force investigation tearing his life apart? His hands clamped together as the anger built. Had she been toying with him when she asked about his past? Bones protested his tightening grip. Had she manipulated events so *he'd* be the one to fly her? Rage swirled in his chest. Did she think the smuggling accusation made him an easy mark?

His throbbing head wanted to explode. The urge to shout "I. Am. Innocent" seethed so hard, he bit the inside of his cheek to leash it.

Something banging into his thigh stopped him from blowing a fuse. Snapping his gaze down, he found Lexi in front of them, staring up at Natasha, her tail whapping his leg. He couldn't tell what the look meant, but Natasha had no problem.

"It's safe." Natasha pivoted left.

Falling in step behind the woman, they managed to wend through the undergrowth with minimal damage. Lexi helped by leading.

Hours or days later—time slowed to molasses—they stopped in front of a downed spruce. The forest had already begun to reclaim the tree. Moss and the surrounding vegetation grew over and around it. To keep from leaving scuff marks, they found a way around the bulk of the wide trunk, then trudged back toward the center where the flora grew dense.

His ribs and head demanded he rest.

Natasha must've felt the same. She carefully knelt within the dead spruce's limbs.

He ungracefully dropped onto more limbs and detritus. Falling backward, he gasped for air. Once he caught his breath, he'd demand answers.

In a minute.

Black spots danced in front of his vision. He'd heard people with concussions shouldn't fall asleep, but that didn't stop his eyes from closing or his mind from replaying the sledgehammer swinging its first strike at his life.

Ian plopped on the barstool at the counter and pulled his cereal bowl closer. Morning sunlight beamed off the granite countertop, forcing him to adjust.

Knock. Knock. Knock.

He snapped his head up, the spoon full of flakes hovering near his mouth.

Pound. Pound. Pound. *"Police! Search warrant. Open up."*

The spoon clattered to the countertop.

"Police. Search warrant."

He clambered off the stool and ran for the front door. Wrenching it open, he found a group of men and women in tactical gear poised on his front porch, sidewalk, and near vehicles with their blue-and-red lights flashing.

A man held out a piece of paper as the rest of the group leveled guns on him. Bulletproof vests that read FBI and Police...

Two birds fiercely squabbling ripped him from the memory. Rubbing his ribs, he couldn't stop the darkness from closing back in. Audible replay of the law enforcement officers asking about a shipment of supplies he'd flown two weeks before blasted, overtaking the forest soundtrack. Blurry mental video crystallized of the officers accusing him of knowing stolen items such as paintings and jewelry were hidden within the boxes.

He was consumed with the inner broadcast, dropping deeper in its hold and sleep.

Chapter Seven

Natasha's eyes flew open, and she blinked. A lot.

Patches of light fought with eerie shapes dancing and swaying overhead. What in the world?

Snuffles and snoring trumpeted in her ear.

Lexi. She'd know that breathing anywhere.

Natasha sneezed. Her chin smacked into something hard *and* soft at the same time; her bruised ribs screamed at the convulsion. Her sinuses filled and she had the urge to sneeze again. Ugh.

With every blink, the mystery shapes overhead turned into towering spruces. She and Dalton had crashed. It all came back to her for the second time in a day. How many times was a person allowed to be unconscious before she worried about brain damage?

A question for another day.

Now she understood the lumpy mattress and lack of city life. Overpowering scents from a variety of trees and vegetation, and swaying flowers of different colors and styles, competed with mold and decay from dead flora. Insects and birds warbled as small animals scurried in and out of sight.

Peace and tranquility. Blah. She missed the frenzied

mishmash of people and technology and the aroma of countless culinary delights filling the air.

The second sneeze ripped free. Yuck. She needed a tissue.

Lifting her left hand took more energy than normal, but she managed to bat at the branch hovering over her throat. The needles jiggled and dropped free, but the branch refused to budge.

She sighed, giving up.

The chaos ruling her mind earlier had dissipated, leaving behind a pounding headache. She'd take it. The ability to think clearly again allowed her to salvage the remnants of her mission and find help.

How long had she been out? Sunlight still peeked through the canopy, but that didn't mean much. Alaska had obscenely long days in the summer. Something like sixteen hours. If she had more energy, she'd check the watch strapped to her right wrist or fumble with a side pocket on her tactical pants for her cell phone. She'd bank on no reception, but the device could still tell time.

The Russians obviously hadn't found them, and she was comfortable believing she, Dalton, and Lexi had evaded the search. They should've been discovered by now. Those men weren't hampered by injuries.

She'd be more anxious and hesitant about her guess if Lexi wasn't asleep. The dog would never allow anyone to creep close without alerting.

Natasha's gaze dropped lower. Through the infernal branch, she spied the soles of muddy boots. The glimpse didn't give her much information other than Dalton remained still.

The trumpeting in Natasha's ear ceased just as badbreath panting began.

"Hey, girl," Natasha crooned.

A wet nose booped her cheek, then a sloppy lick followed. Natasha started to laugh softly, but stopped at the pain in her ribs. She coughed. All her injuries wailed.

"Were you ever going to tell me?"

Snapping her attention forward, she found Dalton wincing and clutching his chest as he sat up. Dirt intermingled with dried blood on his face and beard. At some point he'd lost his sunglasses; she couldn't remember if he'd had them when they escaped. His hat was skewed, his jacket and jeans were filthy, and his knuckles were scraped and bruised. Overall, he looked great for a crash survivor.

Amazing pale green eyes tracked from her boots to her forehead, then narrowed. Pasty skin flushed with color as sparks snapped in his gaze. "Were you?"

"I don't know." The truthful answer made his lips flatten. "To be honest—"

He snorted. "That'd be a first."

A retort flew to her lips, but she wrangled it back. He deserved his anger. "Fair shot."

The lumpy, dead branches beneath her agitated her injuries and she couldn't take it anymore. Sucking in a breath, she utilized her ab muscles to raise her upper body. Slapping her left hand down, twigs and needles dug into her palm. Add the discomfort to the list. The thick branch that hovered at her throat now rested on her shoulder. Whiteness blanketed her vision and her fractured collarbone wailed. Sucking in a breath, she wiggled out of its reach and hung her head. Sweat seeped from everywhere and she hyperventilated.

With too much effort, she managed to slow her breathing and settled against the trunk. In some ways, she felt better, other ways a lot worse. On par for the day.

Once she had her vision back, she refocused on Dalton. "I'm sorry." That needed to be said before anything else. Her father drummed into his three kids' heads: *if you do something wrong, apologize, then make it right.* "I should've introduced myself fully in Whisper."

"You led me to believe you were chasing an abusive boyfriend. Not a police officer tracking a criminal." His jaw clenched. "I thought you had an extreme falling out where the boyfriend fled after he did that to you—" he pointed at her sling "—and you absurdly ran after him."

It wasn't a bad assumption, though her pride balked. Unfortunately, with her years on the force, she'd seen too many domestic situations similar to what he described. And nine times out of ten, the woman stayed with the scumbag.

"You lied to me."

Her mouth dropped open to protest, but he continued, "Omitting details *is* lying. And you failed to disclose *important* facts."

She snapped her jaw closed. He needed to vent. The least she could do was swallow her ego and listen.

"Thanks to you," he continued, "I've lost my only means of income."

That crossed the line. "Uh. No." Her left finger waggled. "*I* did not cause the plane to crash. *Your* landing in a rocky stream did."

"Because *you* paid me to take you to where I dropped my last solo charter," he retorted, leaning to fill the space between them.

"But *I* didn't tell you to attempt that ridiculous landing. *You* did that all on your own."

Pale green irises deepened to jade. Had he moved even closer? Only a foot separated their faces.

"Why did you hire me?"

She blinked at the new line of questioning. "What do you mean?"

"Why me?" The red hue on his skin deepened. "Out of all the bush pilots in Alaska, why *me*?"

This was the second time her intuition warned he hid something important. "Skip sang your praises in Anchorage."

"How did you run into Skip there?"

"Divine intervention."

His expression soured.

"Not a big believer, huh?" She should sit back but couldn't make herself leave the charged space.

"Not anymore." His eyebrows cranked down. "But that's not important."

She disagreed. God was *very* important, but she'd choose a better time for that battle. "Fine. The guy at the front desk of my hotel recommended an airline I hadn't heard of before, located in Anchorage airport. At that counter, I met Skip and his wife. Before I uttered three sentences, Skip led me away from the desk, then told me about you."

Dalton hadn't moved back either. "You alluded you know me." He licked his chapped lips. The white flecks absorbed the moisture, then flaked.

"I know I've seen you before," she corrected. "But I don't know where or how. Were you in the news?"

The red in his cheeks bleached. "We need to get back to the plane."

"Dodging the question makes the answer yes." She racked her brain, but couldn't remember any details. "Why were you in the news?"

"How did the bomb maker hurt you and Lexi? Were you caught in an explosion?"

Her stomach flopped. Unbidden memories tried to surface. "I'm not discussing that now."

His chin jutted. "Then, I'm not discussing anything either."

"Fine." She kept her gaze locked with Dalton's. This battle of wills she planned to win.

Thirty seconds passed.

The muscle in Dalton's jaw ticked. He opened his mouth, then closed it. Frustration leaked into his irises.

She had no real reason not to tell him about the Liberty Bell bombing other than stubborn pride. A flaw she struggled with daily. Yet, if she gave in now, he'd think he could intimidate her in the future. A woman didn't get far in a man's profession by buckling so easily.

Renewed determination had her boring her gaze into his. She. Would. Not. Lose. Especially to a man she almost believed touched her soul. God knew her mission, He wouldn't...

Leaves twisted in the wind, flashing a small patch of sunlight over Ian's eyes. His pale irises weren't solid green. Tiny bands of gold radiated from his pupils. Gorgeous.

The pale green darkened a shade and intensified as he studied her in return.

She swallowed. Now that she was focused on him instead of the ranting in her mind, she couldn't stop seeing him. Not physically but the emotions behind the gaze.

Uncertainty flashed along with confusion.

What was he thinking?

She shifted, suddenly uncomfortable with this contest. "Why does everyone call you Dalton?" The question came out hushed in the charged space between them. She had to create some distance, find a way for him to not see too deeply inside her, too.

He didn't blink, but his eyebrows furrowed. "What?"

"You don't use your first name. Why?" Was it another tool for him to keep people at arm's length?

He shrugged. "It kinda just happened, and since it doesn't bother me, I let it go."

They fell silent again. Her attempt to distract backfired. If anything, she felt more aware of him now.

His pupils widened as surprise flitted in his gaze.

Oh no. What had he seen? What hadn't she hidden? This battle of wills was no longer a game. It was a mining expedition. And she was losing. She didn't need to see him as anything other than a pilot who'd stranded them in the wilds. He had secrets. Ones she intuited were huge and ugly. She didn't need his mess on top of her own drama.

Ian searched her eyes.

Dalton, not Ian. Panic rose. She couldn't think of him as Ian. Stop. Stop thinking. Concentrate on staring him down.

Pain hovered in his pale greens. Physical or emotional? Both? Were his secrets tragic? *Stop. Don't start caring.*

Too late.

She tore her gaze away, losing the contest. Her attention landed on her clenched fist. Ian Dalton was a distraction she could not afford to entertain. She had to remember her priorities.

Lexi panted beside Natasha. Pushing the dog out of the way, she slapped a hand on the ground and struggled to her knees.

"I don't think it's safe to move yet." Dalton placed a hand on the trunk beside her.

"It's fine." Her injuries protested the movement but she had to get away from Dalton.

"How do you know?" he challenged, his tone odd, revealing he was as unbalanced as her. "Did you see any of the men walk past?" The bark on the tree scritched beneath his hand. "Do you have some earpiece thingy that allows you to hear electronic communications? Did they call off the search?"

"One—" her right fingers started to count "—I haven't seen anyone. Two, I'm a police officer, not a spy. The only *earpiece thingy* I own is wireless earbuds. They're great for running, by the way." She adjusted her position to relieve her knees of the twigs gouging her skin. "And three,

I'm sure the area's clear because Lexi is relaxed. She has years of training and experience. No one is close."

His attention shot to the dog, who returned his stare. Lexi sucked in her hanging tongue and cocked her head.

Natasha was about to scream. She needed distance to re-center herself. The battle of wills had revealed more than she'd bargained for, on both sides. "Let's head back to the plane."

Chapter Eight

Ian crowded close to Natasha behind the six-foot-tall Scouler's willow. Not the most comfortable position, but it wasn't wide enough to stand beside her. His jacket brushed against her back while her ponytail bopped his chin.

He was glad for the rest. Even after the long walk back, too much had happened too quickly to process everything. Accusations and responses weren't sinking in. And something had shifted between them during the staring contest. He'd participated in the battle to teach her she couldn't walk all over him, but then the shift happened. She'd shown him vulnerability and distress. He bet she didn't know she pulled back the curtain and revealed the woman behind the badge. And he wasn't foolhardy enough to tell her.

He won the battle, but it felt like he lost. He wasn't the most versed at reading people but he didn't miss the way her hard gaze softened and seemed to see *him*. The part of him that she touched deep within appreciated being seen, but the side of him under investigation wanted to remain unnoticed. He couldn't trust her. He still wasn't 100 percent convinced she hadn't sought him out, but that now seemed more a product of his concussion than reality. If he confided in her, she'd probably just side with all the other law enforcement officers. She'd automatically believe he was guilty without a shred of evidence. Since he'd been accused and had his home searched, he must be a smuggler, right? No. He'd keep avoiding her questions.

He just wished he could escape her in general. Or better yet, had turned her down in Whisper. She was wreaking havoc on his heart. It already beat faster when she was near and constantly tried to sway him to change his stance. To let her in.

Unable to help himself, he inhaled her feminine scent—one he could not figure out—to combat the skunky odor emanating from the full, green shrub. Scouler's willows had great medicinal uses but could make a man choke when the twigs were broken. And the only reason he knew about the healing aspects was because of Skip's wife. The woman doubled as her village's shaman and had a room full of natural remedies. He'd been forced to listen to a long, *long* lecture about the evils of over-the-counter medicine when she caught him swallowing a tablet to fight a headache.

Lexi's tail smacked his thigh, blessedly halting the remnants of that lecture. The dog kept alert, her head swiveling every few seconds.

What did she see or hear?

Unease churned his already-touchy stomach.

Another wind gust struck him, chilling his exposed ears. The temperature had dropped at least ten degrees since this morning, obliterating any sign of summer. If the thermometer kept plunging, he'd have to add snow to their list of miseries.

Peering over Natasha's shoulder, he squinted through the twigs. She'd had them sneak partially down the steep hill, thirty feet from the wreck. The full leaves swayed in the wind, moving enough to show pieces of his plane. Literally. A pang ripped through his heart. The crash had started not long after he first set down. The front landing gear had ripped away, causing the undercarriage to surf the rocks. Bits of metal tore off as it moved, before it smashed into the black spruce, throwing glass and debris wide.

He'd never fly the Cessna again. Grief tightened his chest. So many memories were tied to that plane. His uncle managed to keep it in great condition for forty out of fifty-four years. Five months into Ian's ownership, he'd destroyed it.

The sledgehammer battering his life struck again. With each catastrophic blow, it wasn't a mystery why he'd lost faith in God.

Natasha shifted, altering his thoughts. How could she still have faith? He didn't know her story, but it didn't take a genius to understand something horrible had happened.

A dangling section of the Cessna's fuselage dropped to the ground.

He should be taking pictures for the insurance claim, but instead, he huddled behind a shrub like a fugitive. A criminal. The very label the investigators slapped on him. He'd sunk to an all new low.

Not the time to dwell on the injustice. "The crash was hours ago," he whispered against her ear. "Why are we hiding?"

Her spine snapped straight. "I'm not reckless, that's why." She half turned her head toward him. "We don't know if they left anyone to guard the plane."

Of course he couldn't be stranded without worrying about bomb makers and criminal friends. He wanted to bellow in frustration. His mind supplied a picture of the assault rifles strapped around the men. The weapons didn't make them guilty, but they didn't help Ian's wish the men were innocent sportsmen.

Natasha shifted her weight. "I have no weapon or a team to back me up." She paused. "And I'm out of my jurisdiction."

The weight of his revolver reminded him he was armed.

Not that he'd tell her. He wanted no part of a gunfight. Only in an emergency would he reveal its existence. "So, what was your plan? You flew all this way with no authority—" His gaze narrowed on her face. "Wait. Does your boss know—?"

"Lieutenant, not boss," she snipped.

"Whatever." Another skunk-clearing inhale. If she caught him sniffing her, he was toast. "Question still stands. Does your *lieutenant* know you're here?" His head may be pounding, but something didn't add up. "Why would he send you without help?"

Somehow, her frame grew more rigid.

Lightbulb moment. "You *don't* have permission, do you?" More pieces fell into place. "That's why you hired a bush pilot." He talked more to himself than her. "Alaska has all kinds of official resources who could've flown you—"

"Where?" she retorted. "Until I met you, I had no clue where the bomb maker had set up his rendezvous."

He snorted. "Official resources include the police. They could've helped you interview pilots. You would've eventually talked to me and gotten the location. So, I'm right. You've gone rogue or whatever you call it."

She whirled, though in the tight space, she more flipped against him. "Listen, Dalton." Her hazel eyes tried to fry him. "Just because my lieutenant dismissed my informant's tip doesn't make the information wrong." She poked his chest, his thick coat absorbing the jab. "True, my informant doesn't have the best reputation and he *may* have misinterpreted a rumor or two in the past, but I *knew* the validity of his tip the moment he uttered it."

"Did I touch a nerve?" He couldn't resist the dig.

The fire in her eyes inflamed. "Back off."

Guilt and doubt must have already been niggling her. Only a very dedicated person would fly to this untamed place in her condition on sketchy information from an unreliable source. Or someone with a grudge. Did Natasha seek justice or revenge?

"I'm right, by the way." She shuffled to face the bush.

"You don't know that." He swiped strands of her hair off his chapped lips. He couldn't wait to unload his backpack from the plane. A bottle of water and lip balm were the first items he'd grab.

"I am." She lifted her chin.

Lexi froze, her ears standing tall as she faced forward.

"Dalton, quiet," Natasha commanded so low he barely heard.

Holding his breath, he scouted for a large enough opening in the leaves to see his plane.

Wind toppled smaller pieces of plastic, and an occasional groan echoed from the larger sections shifting.

A rock skittered across the stony ravine.

He stilled. Wind didn't cause that rock to move. Bear? He seriously hoped not. A rabbit was the highest aggression level he and Natasha could handle at the moment.

A low growl rumbled from Lexi's throat.

Natasha rested her hand between the dog's ears and uttered something Ian couldn't hear. The dog ceased growling but remained focused on the plane.

Ian's skin prickled. He couldn't stand the suspense. If the source of the tension didn't reveal itself soon, his racing heart was going to pump right out of his chest.

Another rock joined the first, skittering out of sight.

Just when Ian was about to lose his mind, the top of a bald head appeared. The fuselage hid the man's body, but at least Ian finally had an answer. Human, not bear.

Natasha didn't react to the appearance. She had predicted it.

It rankled that she was right. Well, at least about someone guarding the plane. Ian still clung to the hope that assault-weapon-wielding hunters wanted to find them and not the bomb maker's friends.

The unknown man paced into full view.

Ian's gut churned. This man wasn't outfitted like a harmless gamesman. Black dress pants topped by a black leather jacket adorned the bulky body. Ian couldn't tell how much of the bulk was the man himself or belonged to the layer of sweaters squished into his jacket. His black, rugged boots were the only reasonable clothing for the terrain. No gloves or hat covered the man's hands or head, and his skin had a red tinge. Most likely from the cold instead of a sunburn.

The sudden blaring of a ringtone caused a flock of geese to take off, their honks of displeasure drowning everything.

"...Da," the unknown man stated into a bulky mobile phone.

Ian had never seen that kind of device and wondered if it linked to a satellite. No cell towers existed in the wilds.

A spate of Slavic poured from the guard. By the tone, he didn't like whatever had been said and made it known.

The man was stomping as he paced, vibrating the ground. Another string of the unknown language peppered the air, then he jabbed a finger against the phone.

Wow. The guy really hated whatever was said.

Jamming the phone into his left coat pocket, mystery man marched in another large circle.

Natasha shifted, grabbing Ian's attention.

Her face tilted, revealing worried hazel eyes. "We have to get him away from the plane."

Ian's gaze slid to the obstacle blocking the access to their supplies. "You don't think he's leaving?" Ian didn't, but he wanted to hear Natasha's take on the call. Maybe she understood what was said.

"No." The crease between her brows deepened. "He's too agitated. My guess—he was just told to stay instead of head back to wherever they're holed up."

Ian's shoulders slumped. In this case, he wanted to be wrong.

"So." He scrubbed his face, then grimaced at the blood and grime smearing his palm. "Do we strike up a conversation and hope he's friendly?"

"No way." Her lips flattened. "He's not. He's got to be part of the Russian Mafia meeting the bomb maker."

The blood drained from Ian's head. He swayed, lightheaded. "A bomb maker is working for the Russian *Mafia*?" How did his life go from one catastrophe to the next? First, an investigation accusing him of smuggling; now, he crashed his plane near a bunch of Russians needing bombs.

"I did not sign up for this," he wheezed, squeezing his eyes shut. The dizziness worsened. He popped his eyelids open and glared at the source of his latest misery. "Lady, you are out of your mind. You knew a *bomb* maker was meeting with the *Mafia* and you came here *alone*?"

Her chin snapped up. "I'm *not* alone."

"I. Don't. Count." He exaggerated each word. If she thought—

"I was referring to Lexi." Her left finger jabbed toward the dog. "But, good to know you have my back."

He bent his knees, ignoring the protest from the joints. Staring straight into her eyes, he whispered, "If you think guilting me is going to work, you're going to be sadly disappointed. I'm not part of your scheming."

She met his gaze squarely. "Guess what, *Ace*. You're up to your elbows in *my scheming*. You *have* to help me. As you pointed out, the wilds don't have airports, and I doubt they have cell towers either. I bet there isn't a village for *miles*. You either work with me to call in help or embrace a new survivalist lifestyle."

Chapter Nine

Natasha stewed. If she could pace, she'd form a trench in the ground.

Who did he think he was? Her left hand clenched into a fist. Granted, he wasn't a trained professional, and he hadn't known he was part of her reconnaissance mission, but still.

She smashed against him as she ungracefully whirled.

Hard, green eyes lasered on her. "Let me guess, you just realized you forgot to tell me some other significant detail to ruin my life."

Her teeth ground together. Unclamping her jaw, she glared at him. "No. We need to talk about how we're going to search the plane." Her slinged arm pressed against his jacket. "Unless recovering our supplies is too much of *my scheming* for you to handle."

His chapped lips flattened. "You want me to apologize but I'm not going to." He lowered his head. "You withheld important facts, *Officer* Greene. I'm allowed to be angry about your duplicity."

She flushed. "You're right." The words tasted bitter. She hated making mistakes. "But can you put your anger aside long enough to help me check out the plane?"

He straightened. "It'll be faster if I go by myself."

She opened her mouth—

"Your injuries slow you down." He raised a hand. "Don't blast me. It's the truth."

Her mouth snapped closed.

"I know my plane better than you." He peered between the Scouler's willow twigs. "You stay here." Without waiting for her response, he skulked to the black spruce at the edge of the stream.

Lexi whined, her tail swishing at an impressive rate. Big brown eyes implored Natasha to follow Dalton.

"I have to stay here." She scratched between the dog's ears. Those words burned in her mouth. Dalton did not have to be so blunt about her inability to sneak.

He inched to the edge of the branch coverage. His smashed Cessna rested on the other side of the tree.

Guilt squeezed her chest. While the actual crash wasn't her fault, she did own some of the blame. Did that mean she had to offer reimbursement? Probably. But she'd only be responsible for a small percentage, not the whole price tag. Even with that, it'd probably wipe out her savings. Indignation gobbled the guilt. He could have landed somewhere else, or told her they had to come back tomorrow. To hold her completely accountable was outrageous.

The unmistakable sound of a lighter flaring ripped her out of her rant. The guard stood in the center of the rock bed, ignoring the water rushing over his boots. That water had to be icy, but maybe he was used to arctic temperatures. She didn't know much about the Russian climate, but she always figured some parts of the country remained frigid.

A cigarette dangled between red-tinged fingers. Twice, the lighter's flame extinguished in the gusting wind. He turned his back and managed to light the white roll, puffing avidly to keep the end burning.

Gross. Clapping her left hand over her nose and mouth,

she blocked the nasty smell. Wetness coated the side of her palm and she yanked it away. *Ewww.* Blood and dirt. Great. No wonder her head throbbed. With so many other body aches, she hadn't bothered to check on her face.

Dalton dropped into a crouch.

Natasha held her breath. So far, he'd managed to evade detection.

He hustled around the spruce to the cockpit's opened door.

Had they left it open or had the Russians searched the plane? Probably both.

Lexi's ears twitched, and she stepped forward.

Anxiety gripped them both.

The Russian studied the end of his dwindling cigarette while blowing out a cloud of noxious fumes.

Dalton duck-walked down the length of the bent fuselage, stopping when he reached the cargo hold. He lifted the small door easily, too easily. She doubted the sturdy latch popped open in the crash. Her guess: the Russians had searched the space and hadn't bothered securing it after.

That didn't bode well.

He peered over his shoulder, toward her hiding spot. He shook his head, his face pinched and red.

Her heart plunged as fury took over. They stole her luggage. All her clothes and toiletries, not to mention the satellite phone her credit card had winced at purchasing, gone. By the grace of God, she had her IDs in one of her pants' pockets, but she'd counted on that phone to save them.

Lexi growled, her body arrowed to charge forward.

"Eh?" the Russian called, searching the hill. "'ello?" He dropped the cigarette into the stream, not caring that he littered as it whisked out of sight.

Dalton froze, his palms on the side of the fuselage.

His gaze darted between Natasha and the threat on the other side.

She had to distract the guard. Give Dalton time to escape. "Lexi, bait." She signed the word, signaling to play the game they had made up together to keep their skills fresh.

The dog took off, then instantly slowed on account of her injured leg.

Grief shredded Natasha's heart. She asked too much from her partner. Tears crowded the corners of Natasha's eyes, but she couldn't let them fall. Dalton needed help.

Natasha shuffled to the edge of the tall bush. The Russian's gaze had shifted, hopefully following Lexi's noisy trajectory.

Natasha stepped into the open and motioned for Dalton to stay put.

He nodded, not moving an inch.

"'ello?" the guard asked again, taking one step, then another away from the plane. "Pasha?" A litany of Russian followed the name.

She didn't understand a single word.

Keep moving, buddy.

The man cautiously strode upstream. He grabbed the HK433 slung across his back—highly illegal to own—and swung the assault rifle into place by its strap.

Oh, Lord, she prayed. This had gone from distraction to potential disaster in a blink.

"Pilot?" the guard called, his Russian accent thick. Fitting the butt of the rifle into his shoulder, he scanned the hill farther up the ravine.

Natasha motioned for Dalton to crouch low and run.

He bolted.

She lost years of her life in the seconds it took Dalton to dash to the other side of the spruce. He knelt and grabbed his heaving chest.

Was he having a heart attack? "Dalton," she hissed, trying to keep the guard in sight at the time.

He waved her off. "Ribs," he wheezed.

Brrrrr-brr-brrrr-brrrrrrrr. The automatic HK433 opened fire.

Natasha dropped to the ground. Her hands automatically raised to cover her head. Her vision blacked at the agony from her fractured right collarbone.

Thunks drilled into tree trunks and the surrounding ground while the Cessna's body screeched at the barrage of bullets.

Her mind wailed in pain and for Lexi.

The gunfire stopped and a deluge of Russian poured from the guard.

Her training kicked in. She had to get Dalton and Lexi away from here. If this man didn't put a bullet in their heads, the sound of gunfire would have his buddies swarming soon.

The shrub's stems were too thick and numerous to see through from this vantage on the ground. Boots skittered rocks and vibrated the earth, but Natasha couldn't tell if the guard moved closer.

Tears coated her cheeks. Fishing out a napkin she had shoved into her pocket from one of the airport layovers, she wiped her nose. She had to master the pain. Dalton and Lexi relied on her expertise to survive. Not that she'd been in many—two—situations involving gunmen intent on killing. Then she'd had trained officers at her back and more at her disposal.

Swallowing the nausea riding at the top of her throat, she forced herself to focus. First, she had to assess the situation. She used the Scouler's willow branches to maintain her balance as she struggled to stand. Her legs shook; two parts adrenaline, one part exhaustion. Cold wind drove her damp pants to cling to her legs. A minor misery in the scheme of things.

Finding an opening in the twigs and leaves, she studied the scene. Dalton lay curled with his hands over his head. The spruce still hid him from the guard. She exhaled. One safe. Now to find her partner.

Lexi remained out of sight.

The Russian, however, prowled, glaring at the slope. The barrel of the HK433 poised to fire again.

If she moved now, the guard would spot her instantly. Blowing out a breath, she racked her brain. She needed another distraction. One that didn't cause the gunman to call in the troops—if they weren't already on their way.

The Russian marched to the plane. He kicked a piece of debris out of his path and rounded the tail. The rifle barrel followed everywhere he visually searched.

She'd never escape clean. This guy had too much trigger-happy vigilance.

Switch to Plan B. Disable the guard and take him out of the equation. Not permanently, but incapacitate his ability to do anything against them.

The rifle swung with the Russian's sudden whirl. He inspected her section of hill.

Natasha froze, not daring to breathe or blink.

A low, menacing growl somewhere to her left raised the hairs on her neck. She'd never heard that sound from Lexi. Had a bear or wolf joined the party? The situation was deteriorating fast. *Lord, help us.*

The Russian gripped his rifle tighter and carefully side-stepped up the slope.

No. Her heart battered against her ribs. Two more steps and he'd find Dalton.

The low growl rumbled again.

The guard didn't stop.

Natasha's palm protested at strangling a branch. She

had to protect the innocent: Dalton. "Don't shoot," she yelled. Blood rushed in her veins, roaring past her ears.

The Russian halted, fixating his rifle on her shrub.

Dalton's arms lowered as he swiveled his face up toward her.

"Don't shoot," she called again. "I'm unarmed." Did the Russian comprehend English?

"Come out," the guard demanded, all his focus toward her.

Dalton shook his head and mouthed "don't."

She had to. This got her closer to neutralizing the threat without endangering a civilian. "I'm injured."

"Eh?" His barrel didn't twitch.

He had steady nerves. That was good. Sort of. Anxiety caused twitchy trigger fingers.

Lord, help me, please. She trudged from behind the tall willow.

Chapter Ten

Ian couldn't breathe. Horror coexisted with terror, freezing his muscles.

Natasha either had a concussion that blocked common sense or she took her job a little too seriously. Why else would she confront a man who had just unloaded a hail of bullets into a wrecked plane?

Cold sweat oozed through Ian's pores, and his heart strained to pump iced blood. He needed to move, do something, but he couldn't even twitch. His locked body didn't care about the humiliation it caused. Primal instincts ruled.

He couldn't see the gunman, but he got an excellent view of the automatic weapon aimed at Natasha. Never in his life had he been this close to a deadly machine gun. The black matte finish bore scratches and marks.

Hysteria gripped his mind. He shouldn't be close enough to know that. *Oh, God, help.* Ian hoped God decided to listen. Maybe He'd offer some of that divine intervention Natasha had talked about.

The reckless woman slowly stepped into view.

Pity strangled some of the panic. Until this moment, he hadn't really paid attention to the entire package of injuries. The plane wreck had added new bruises and cuts to her exposed skin. Dirt, mud, berry juice, and who-knew-

what-else stained the damp clothes hanging limply on her
broken frame.

"Pilot?" the Russian asked, his gun not wavering an
inch.

Another low, ominous growl resounded through the
tense silence. Lexi? The hairs on Ian's body stood. Wolf?
Primordial instincts strangling his throat tightened. One
wolf meant more lurked nearby.

The Russian scoffed. "You not pilot."

Get. Up, Ian's conscience screamed. *Help the woman.*
"I am," he croaked, sitting up. Clearing his throat, he tried
again. "I'm the pilot."

The weapon pivoted and Ian starred into the round hole
of death. A blurry image of the guard hustling to clear the
tree registered in the background. He couldn't stop staring
at the dark end of the rifle.

"Don't move." The Russian kept his gun trained on Ian
while he peered up and to the left. "You," he barked at Natasha. "Come down. Slowly."

"That's the only speed I have," she quipped, completely
composed.

Ian's mouth was as dry as a desert and he had trouble
stringing two thoughts together, while Natasha bantered
with a killer. He was in over his head and sinking fast.

With every labored step Natasha made, Ian castigated
himself for quivering like a scared little boy. He had to
take a page from the infuriatingly brave woman and stand
against the threat. He had never thought of himself as
weak, and he didn't want to start now.

Trained police officer or not, Natasha needed a partner right now, not a victim adding to the danger. Latching on to the adrenaline, he slapped a hand on the ground
and pushed upward. His ribs protested the movement. He
grimaced but kept going until he stood.

The Russian glared at Ian. "I tell don't move."

A sinister growl somewhere behind Ian had him freezing. *Please be a very angry Lexi.* "Natasha?"

For some reason, Ian raised his hands in surrender. Like that would ward off an animal attack.

"Don't move." Natasha stared at something behind him. Her face lost color and she froze partway down the hill.

The assault rifle shifted to Ian's right. The Russian sighted down the barrel.

Time slowed.

Natasha yelled, "Run!"

His world resembled a movie playing one frame a minute.

The Russian squeezed the trigger.

Piercing explosions from the rifle pierced his ears.

Ian threw himself sideways, slamming into the spruce's branches. Needles and twigs dug into his body, scraping every piece of skin they could find. He pushed against the tree holding him back. Tangling in the swaying branches, he tripped, trying to rush forward.

Time snapped back to normal, then sped up.

Malevolent growls and yips responded to the barrage of bullets.

The Russian let out a continuous primal roar as he fired an onslaught of lead at the unknown threat.

Ian found his footing, finally breaking free of the tree. He had no plan. No thoughts other than *run, run, run*. Racing around the Russian, he bolted up the hill toward Natasha. His heart pumped in his throat and he couldn't swallow.

She stumbled, a boot catching on a swatch of blueberry bushes. She threw her arms out for balance.

He lengthened his stride, climbing faster.

She yelped as she snapped her sling back down.

Just as she pitched forward, he managed to dart in front.

Without thinking, he grabbed the bicep closest to him and wrapped his other arm around her.

She screamed as her weight smashed into him, almost knocking him down. Digging his boots into the loam, he absorbed the force, determined to keep them upright. He may have yelled along with her, thanks to her slinged arm burrowing into his ribs.

Loud breaths sawed in and out of her mouth, and he joined the chorus. His gaze slid beyond the Russian and he almost lost his bladder.

A gray-and-white wolf bared its teeth, jumping and dodging the bullets tearing holes into leaves, branches, and ground.

Ian cranked his neck, wildly searching every direction. Where were the others? If he remembered correctly, one wolf showed itself, then herded the prey toward the rest of the awaiting pack.

A second growl rumbled from above.

Snapping his gaze upward, he froze. Another gray-and-white wolf stood at the top of the steep hill, staring at the Russian. It was too far to see the color of the animal's eyes, but they shifted to appraise Ian and Natasha.

Fear replaced the blood in Ian's body. His worst nightmare had come to life: crashing his plane in the middle of nowhere and being mauled by wild animals.

Frenzied male shouts broke through his horrifying imaginings of the wolves attacking. Fresh rounds of automatic fire ripped through the charged air.

"Oh no," Natasha wheezed, bunching his jacket into her tightening fist. "More Russians."

Ian twisted. Sure enough, two men inappropriately dressed for the terrain charged down the other hill. Brass casings from expended bullets flew out of the top of automatic rifles as their fingers firmly pressed triggers.

"We have to get out of here." He searched the only direction free from threats. So far, it remained clear. But was that a ruse the wolves had set up?

His gaze swept the entire area again. The second wolf was gone. The first darted into the tall foliage, disappearing.

A third growl hailed from the space that had been empty a second ago.

Before Ian could register the latest round of danger, a black-and-brown streak rushed past, a few feet below his and Natasha's position. The gait wasn't even, but Lexi made it work.

Air sucked through Natasha's teeth and she stiffened.

The dog charged at the guard on their side of the hill.

Lowering his weapon a few inches, the Russian started to turn in their direction when the dog launched.

Lexi sunk her teeth into the Russian's forearm, tearing it away from the gun. With a violence Ian had never witnessed, she shook the guard and took him to the ground.

The guard screamed, the pitch so high chills skittered down Ian's spine. A string of Russian poured from the man as he attempted to hit the dog.

Lexi shook the guard again and pulled, avoiding the blows. The man's leather jacket lost the battle to sharp teeth.

"Dalton," Natasha croaked. "Get the gun."

"What?" He snapped straight. "I'm not going anywhere near that dog."

"She won't attack you." Natasha pushed herself off him, then shoved his chest. "We need a weapon." She pushed again. "Hurry. Before the others catch up."

Sweat broke out all over and he tripped over berry shrubs. More adrenaline flooded him, making him clumsy and his thoughts slow. Trying not to think too hard about interrupting an attacking dog, he hustled to the downed pair.

"Lexi, hold," Natasha commanded.

The dog growled, her teeth still sunk into the Russian, who hadn't stopped shouting and thrashing.

His compatriots also bellowed. A new round of bullets sawed the air, but the spruce sheltered Ian and Lexi from harm.

Ian slammed to his knees, inches from the man's hips. The guy tried to punch Ian, but Ian caught the slow fist and wrestled it to the ground.

"Stop." Ian wrenched his revolver free of its holster but didn't point it at the Russian. *Never aim if you aren't prepared to shoot.* His father's words echoed in his chaotic mind.

The guard stilled, his nearly black eyes radiating hatred.

"I'm taking the rifle." Ian motioned to the weapon laying half on the Russian. With clumsy fingers, he unsnapped the clasp on the butt of the rifle and pulled the sling from beneath the man's back.

The Russian twitched.

Lexi growled.

A weird lump in the guard's leather jacket jogged Ian's memory. The satellite phone. He jammed his Smith & Wesson back in the holster and dug into the man's pocket, freeing the device. It was a lot heavier than he'd expected.

"Dalton."

Natasha's shout spurred him into action. Leaping up, he hugged the pilfered items and ran.

Chapter Eleven

"Say that again," Randy demanded, smashing the satellite phone against his ear. Between the gusting wind and the Russian-accented English, he couldn't understand a word.

"Dog attacked Vanya," the Mafia criminal, Andrei, repeated, hysteria evident.

"A dog?" Randy rubbed his forehead to soothe the forming migraine.

Pasha set the large spool of detonation wire, aka det wire, beside a white spruce and ambled toward Randy. After the man returned from raiding the plane, he'd helped Randy haul the supplies needed to secure the hideout's perimeter.

"*Da.* Dog," Andrei shouted. "Vanya bleeding. Need hospital."

Randy was missing something important. "Where did the dog come from?"

"Nowhere. Just appeared."

Randy blinked. He doubted the area had a pack of wild dogs; he'd have heard them by now. Only one explanation made sense. Yet, not really. The bush pilot who flew him hadn't had a dog on their flight.

"…no," Andrei shouted, but the wind took his words. "…woman…man."

Randy's gut tightened. *Two* invaders. Less than a mile from his hideout. Coincidence or compromised?

"…wolves."

He dug his fingers deeper into his aching forehead. "Wolves?" The longer Andrei talked, the less he made sense.

Pasha stiffened, his eyebrows slamming down as he faced the crash's general direction.

"*Da.* We shoot at them." Vivid streams of Russian hailed in the background on Andrei's side. "Dog attack. Vanya need hospital."

Randy couldn't listen to another word. He'd find out what happened later. "Andrei, bring Vanya here."

"I help," Pasha announced, marching toward his HK433 resting against a trunk.

"No," Randy snapped. They weren't finished setting up the traps, and Randy needed at least one Russian for protection.

"What?" Andrei asked. "You no want me bring Vanya?"

"Pasha, you stay," Randy barked, then into the phone he ordered, "Andrei, bring Vanya here. Have Pyotr escort the man and woman—"

"They gone."

Steam nearly blew from Randy's ears. "You're just telling me this *now*?"

"*Da.* Vanya need hospital."

If Andrei stated that one more time, he'd ensure the Russian spent quality time in his own bed beside his comrade.

"Send Pyotr after them," he shouted, the phone biting into his clenched fingers. *"Now."*

Natasha desperately needed to slow down.

They had fled the open, hilly area using the rocky ravine, plunging into the forest a half mile from that spot. The steep hills abated into uneven terrain as the stream twisted somewhere out of sight. Towering trees blurred as she did her best to run. The undergrowth and dead debris made it nearly impossible to find her footing. It kept hiding pitfalls and objects such as stones and roots while also trying to trip her.

Ian crashed through the forest right behind her, with Lexi by his side.

Natasha's lungs burned. The chemicals from the trap in Philadelphia that had broken her body had also damaged her organs. She had a fifty-fifty chance of recovery, but Lexi did not. The lung damage for her was permanent. The German shepherd had been forced to retire and that left Natasha floundering. She couldn't imagine going to work without her partner. The lieutenant promised she could train with another dog if she wanted to remain in the K-9 unit, but she had put off the decision.

Adrenaline fueled Natasha's flight but didn't mask enough of the pain. Sheer determination to escape trigger-happy Russians kept her going, but if they didn't slow down soon, she and Lexi were going to collapse.

Dalton probably itched to leave the K-9 team behind. The man had nothing wrong with *his* lungs. He could outrun them easily, and yet, he hadn't.

"I don't…" she wheezed. "Know…where… I'm…" Rib-wracking cough. "Going."

Nausea rode high in her throat. Oxygen barely circulated in her abused brain. If the black-and-white lights dancing in her vision were any indication, she was on the verge of fainting.

"Stop for a second," Dalton gasped, his breathing ragged. Maybe he was struggling more than Natasha had realized.

She halted, struggling to breathe. *Oh, Lord,* she prayed,

swaying. The flashes in her vision competed with the nausea that competed with passing out.

"We can't keep running." Dalton's chest rose and fell, and the HK433 and satellite phone cradled in his arms made her dizzier with the motions.

Lexi hung her head. Her tongue lolled out of her panting mouth and she gagged.

"Can we hide?" Natasha searched for a place. An abundance of trees and underbrush met her gaze. The urgency to move gripped her again, her legs itching to start running. Her body threatened mutiny if she did.

"We have to." He scanned the environment. "Wish we could climb—"

She snorted. "Not on a good day would you find me scaling a tree." She pointed at herself. "City girl through and through. Bad guys and guns are my department." She motioned to Dalton. "I need your help in the woods."

It hurt her pride to admit she had a failing, but her and Lexi's survival depended on Natasha knowing her limits. And she was a far cry from Daniel Boone.

Dalton shifted the bounty. "Thank you."

Natasha blinked, unsure the reason for the thanks. His eyes no longer bore hard shards…that had to mean something positive, right?

"I mean, for saving me." He inhaled. "When you confronted that guard, I couldn't believe you'd risk your life for me."

The urge to shrug off his gratitude and hide behind her job was strong, but for some reason, she couldn't force out the platitude. "You wouldn't be in this mess if it wasn't for me." She cleared her throat at the unexpected honesty. "And, uh, you helped me too. So, yeah. We're even."

Flashes of him running up the hill to catch her when the chaos erupted replayed.

Wind shook the evergreen needles and whacked long

branches together. Had it gotten colder? She shivered. Clouds still obscured the sun, darkening the already-gloomy forest.

Now wasn't the time to unpack all the emotions swirling in the space. "How far have we run?"

"Not far enough." Dalton pivoted to search. "I keep thinking one of those Russians are going to pop out from behind a tree any second."

"Me too." Another shiver shook her. "I can't keep up that pace."

"Come on." Dalton turned to the left. "Follow my lead and try not to damage the shrubs."

Yes, sir, she groused inwardly. "Lexi, follow." Natasha motioned for the dog to go next.

She'd only taken two steps when twigs snapping beyond their movements reached her.

Foreboding slithered down her spine and she halted. "Dalton," she hissed. "Something's coming."

He whirled, the rifle's sling flying outward, then slapping his back. "You hear it?" he whispered, darting his gaze everywhere.

"Yes."

Lexi's head jerked upright and her tongue sucked back into her mouth. A low growl rumbled from her throat.

"Wolf?" She paled at the memory of the savage beast too close behind Dalton. On TV, wolves were majestic. In real life, they were terrifying.

Dalton blanched. "Could be." His whisper trembled. "They might not have run far."

Her stomach shriveled. *Lord, we still need Your protection.*

Vibrations from steady thumps echoed closer.

"That's no wolf." Dalton craned his neck toward the ground they had covered.

Bear? Or equally bad, human?

"Hide. Now."

"Where?" she hissed, bending as if that helped. She didn't accomplish anything but causing pain.

Dalton didn't answer. He dashed behind the closest evergreen.

Natasha signed for Lexi to follow him.

The dog took off as Natasha fought with the resurgence of adrenaline making her inept. She had training to handle the increased epinephrine, but she wasn't in top physical condition right now. She did her best to not leave a trail behind as she headed for the tree.

"Nat, hurry up," Dalton whisper-yelled.

"Do *not* call me Nat," she puffed, finally ducking behind the wide-bottomed evergreen. "*Never* call me Nat. I'm not an insect."

Dalton slapped a hand over her mouth.

Her jaw dropped to bite him.

He pressed his lips against her ear. "Listen."

She froze, not easy to do with starving lungs on fire for air.

Two seconds later, twigs cracked, branches swished, and footsteps thumped.

Not a bear or a wolf. The Russians had caught up.

Chapter Twelve

Ian removed his hand from Natasha's mouth. The poor woman could barely catch a breath and he wasn't much better. Between himself, the dog, and Natasha, the threat on the other side could zero right in on them.

Heavy footsteps stopped.

Tense silence permeated the space. Insects and birds quieted, amplifying the wind swishing the leaves and needles.

Natasha's unique scent competed with the cloying aroma of sap, bark, evergreen needles, and dead detritus littering the forest floor. He couldn't stop himself from drawing in another inhale.

Her essence shattered some of the panic overriding his thinking. *Run, run, run,* had been his prevailing thought for too long. The concussion hadn't helped, fueling his inability to reason clearly. But he needed to stop reacting and start planning. Natasha admitted she needed him to help her survive just like he needed her to combat the Russians. They could aid each other if they could get past their issues. And that was a big *if.* Anger warmed his insides like a blanket.

Regardless of their status, shelter, food, water, and a way to call for help topped his survival list. But first, they had to deal with the latest round of danger. Apparently, they hadn't had enough already.

Juggling the rifle and phone, he tugged his coat sleeve up, and dug his fingernail into the tiny ridge on the side of his watch. A small compass swiveled out from its hiding place against the stainless steel. Noting the direction of the downed plane, he tucked the compass away. Knowing the plane's direction didn't help them. The Russians had stripped it of *everything*: his gear, the rifle he kept stashed for wildlife, and the emergency supply pack. They'd even destroyed his radio, but for some reason, he found comfort in believing he could find the Cessna again.

Carefully spreading a few branches, he searched for the owner of the footsteps.

In a sick way, he wished a bear or wolf loomed nearby. Those threats could be handled without violence, if done right. But no, at least one Russian followed their trail.

"Zhenshchina," the man called. "I know you here, woman."

Natasha stiffened, her left hand buried in the fur between Lexi's ears.

Similar to the Cessna guard, this guy hadn't dressed appropriately for the wilderness. A black leather jacket with a black fur collar topped black dress pants that covered thick black shoes. No hat or gloves protected his blond hair or the reddening fingers clutching an assault rifle that matched the one Ian had stripped off the downed Russian.

"You hurt Vanya." Mafia Two, aka MT, pivoted, scanning the trees three feet to their left.

Vanya? Was that the name of the Russian Lexi attacked?

"You no hide," MT continued his one-sided conversation.

Yes, we hide.

MT slowly panned his rifle. "You with man?"

Natasha clasped Ian's forearm, tugging.

He leaned closer.

"Let's back away as quietly as possible," she whispered so softly the puffs of air against his cheek seemed louder. "He's going to find us if we stay."

"Agreed." He had been about to suggest the same thing.

Needing his hands free, he struggled to snap the sling clasp back onto the butt of the rifle. Natasha snatched the satellite phone from his hand. The clasp locked in place and he slung the weapon over his head, situating it against his back. The weight and the death it portended sat on his heart like an anvil.

She slid the bulky phone inside her sling.

The hairs rose on the back of his neck, warning him time had almost run out.

"Pilot," the Russian shouted again, too close for Ian's liking. "Woman."

"Why couldn't I be the pilot?" she grumbled. "Sexist pig."

Plodding forward, Ian did his best not to step on the myriad of branches, twigs, and leaves covering the ground. Some places grew more vegetation than others. The trees, as well, had no rhyme or reason. Some sections were thick while others were thin to the point of creating odd-shaped clearings.

Scouting forward didn't have 100 percent of his focus as he tried to keep tabs on the Russian.

Lexi trotted ahead, snatches of her tail the only visible piece at times.

"Eh!" the Russian yelled.

Adrenaline sliced through Ian's bloodstream.

"Dalton," Natasha puffed from behind.

"Do you see him?" He dodged around a thicket of intermeshed shrubs.

"Movement."

He started to run. He had hoped the guy chose a different direction, but the vegetation worked against them. Too much foliage snapped, slapped, and tangled, destroying their attempts at stealth, and obscured the man from view.

Natasha's boots tromped a few feet back. Speed over guile became their priority.

The uneven terrain didn't help. Roots, small boulders, and rocks hid beneath the detritus. Every now and then, they protruded, warning him of their existence. Gashes in the ground gave no indication of their danger nor did the furrows made by animals. So far, he'd managed to stay on his feet, but for how long? He played a risky game of vegetation roulette. It was only a matter of time before he lost.

Ducking around a healthy Sitka spruce, he hustled.

"Can Lexi attack?" The words stole precious air from his starving lungs.

"Yes, but she shouldn't have before without my command," Natasha answered, closer than before. She had caught up.

"I'm not complaining." Instead of his boot hitting the ground, it dropped into a hole to midshin. He pitched forward.

Natasha tried to grab him, but his weight and momentum worked against her. She lost her grip and landed in a prickly rosebush rising from a mass of ferns. Pink flowers shook and danced, shedding their petals on top of her.

Ian slapped his hands on the ground, saving his face from meeting a moldy, dead branch.

Natasha yelped as Lexi dashed into their space. The dog sniffed its owner, who whimpered and sucked in air.

Noisy footsteps crashing through vegetation grew louder every second.

Ian yanked and pulled, but his boot refused move. *Come. On*, he mentally yelled, trying to twist his ankle and pull at the same time. Stuck. He grabbed behind his knee, and his biceps strained to help. Centimeter by agonizing centimeter his boot fought against the dirt locking it in place. Whatever animal dug this hole deserved to become dinner tonight. If he lived long enough to catch it.

"Ha!" a male voice crowed. "I see you, *zhenshchina*."

Lexi growled, standing in front of Natasha.

Ian doubled his efforts to free his foot.

Natasha groaned. Fern leaves partially covering her shook and rustled. She placed her left hand on the ground and pushed upward.

Ian's boot only had a few more inches to go.

"Stay freeze," MT demanded, breaking through another copse of prickly rosebushes and ferns to Ian's back left. The Russian fixed his assault rifle on Lexi.

The German shepherd bared her teeth and growled.

MT paled and visibly trembled. "Dog no attack *me*." His expression darkened. "I shoot you both." His gun flicked to Natasha. "You send dog attack Vanya."

Unmitigated rage roared through Ian. This guy planned to kill a dog and a defenseless woman? *Scumbag.* Without thinking through his actions, Ian snatched up the thick dead branch devoid of leaves. He bellowed as he tore his boot free and swung the wood like a baseball bat.

MT started to react, but the branch reached him first. It struck his gun, then chest, knocking the criminal backward.

Going with the momentum, Ian continued moving with the swing, into a circle. He whirled around like a discus thrower and smashed the branch against the Russian's chest again.

MT fell, slamming onto his back.

Red hazed Ian's vision and he charged forward. Imitating a pro golfer, he swung, connecting against the rifle, but it didn't go very far. The sling kept it strapped to the man. That enraged him more. Another war cry tore from his aching throat and he lifted the wood—

"Dalton!"

The shout halted his swing at its peak.

"Stop," Natasha commanded.

Ian snapped his gaze up to find her struggling with the ferns. The red tinge bled from his vision and he blinked.

"Lexi, guard."

The dog growled again and trotted forward.

Piercing pain in Ian's ribs and stabbing agony in his brain woke him from the last vestiges of rage. He staggered backward. What had he been about to do? He opened his hands and the branch bounced on the ground. He'd never felt so savage in his life. Clutching his racing heart, he searched the ground without really seeing it. What had he done? Oh no. What had he done?

"It's okay, Ian," Natasha soothed.

"No, it's not." He stared at the branch.

"You saved Lexi," she continued, "and me."

Had he?

His gaze drifted forward. MT lay unmoving, the back of his head against a protruding tree root.

Ian croaked and dropped to his knees. "Is he dead?" His fingers shook so hard it took him two tries to worm them between the man's black fur collar and skin. Holding his breath, he felt for a pulse.

Blood pumped steadily beneath his fingers. Knocked out. Not dead.

Ian slumped to the ground and exhaled.

"Search him," Natasha demanded.

The relief seized. Reality sledgehammered the bubble of adrenaline-fueled giddiness as he realized just how close he'd come to participating in murder. Self-defense, sure, but he would have been responsible for the guy's death all the same.

Black spots crowded his vision as the forest began to blur. Was he about to pass out? The lightheadedness said yes.

Chapter Thirteen

The blood drained from Ian's face and he swayed.

He's going down. Natasha had to get to him before the shock turned serious.

She railed against her broken/fractured bones, fuzzy head, and wailing ribs preventing her from easily leaping forward. Maneuvering to her knees, she batted at the ferns smacking her face. Holding her sling against her abdomen, she used her left arm and knees to crawl forward as fast as she could. Her kneecaps ground against twigs and branches, threatening to be the next broken body parts.

Lexi remained beside the Russian, her gaze never shifting. Once she had a command, she'd only break it under extreme circumstances. Natasha crawling on the ground wasn't even a blip on that scale, so Lexi continued to guard.

"Good girl," Natasha wheezed, finally reaching the Russian's sprawled legs.

Ian's swaying increased.

She crawled over the attacker's shins as a shortcut. "I've got you."

Glassy eyes didn't register her statement.

Climbing over the second leg, she plopped in front of Ian. "You're okay." Her left palm cupped his clammy cheek. "This is normal."

Memories of her first weeks on the job filtered through her mind. Those days had been rough and she'd questioned if she was cut out to be a city police officer. The atrocities she witnessed gave her nightmares, and if she hadn't had a strong, veteran partner, she'd have quit. Big Mike had been her rock, and now she'd be the same for Ian.

"Dalton, look at me."

Two blinks.

Progress. He heard her. "Ian," she continued, "look at me."

More blinks. His body trembled, constantly shivering. Seconds passed, then those bleary eyes tracked to her.

"That's it." She stroked his cheek, feeling guilty for the dirt smearing his skin. "This is normal. You're okay. Your body's processing the adrenaline." Idle chatter usually worked to calm a chaotic mind, gave it something else to focus on. "He didn't hurt anyone. You're fine. I'm fine. Lexi's fine. You did what you had to do. You saved us."

Bit by bit, the glassiness receded from his haunted eyes.

"Let me know if you need to puke." She smiled. "That's normal too," she added so he didn't think she made fun of him.

"You. Puke?"

And he's back from Shockland. "Sure." A memory rose. "The last time was a doozy." She shuddered. "I was six hours into my shift and I ate a chicken sandwich from this hole-in-the-wall restaurant. By the griminess, I should've walked out, but I was too hungry and only had a few minutes to grab food before I got another call." She shook her head. "I paid for that decision for four days."

A greenish tinge mingled with the pasty-white skin. "I'm—"

He twisted out of her grip and lost whatever he'd eaten earlier, next to the Russian's hip.

Natasha switched to breathing through her mouth so she didn't join him, then rubbed his back.

He jerked. Reaching behind, he weakly tried to bat her away.

No touching. Got it. She retracted her arm.

Convulsing heaves wracked him. More dry than ejecting anything in his stomach.

She winced in empathy for him and pity for her. Everything hurt.

"Oh, God, why," he moaned, bending deeper.

"He's listening." Natasha prayed for them both to find the strength to make it through the next few minutes. If she didn't pass out from the pain, the concussion pounding her head would do the trick.

"He's—" huge inhale "—turned His back on me." Ian spit.

"I disagree." She didn't want to argue but couldn't let that statement go.

He wiped his mouth with the back of his hand. His other palm smeared the dirt—now mud—from the tears brought on by puking. "I lost—" he cleared his throat "—my faith when He disowned me."

She bit her lip; now wasn't the time to argue theology. The topic distracted him though. Color returned to his skin and she'd take that as a win.

A wrinkled napkin emerged from his coat and he blew his nose.

"Sounds like we're going to have a rousing debate."

"No thanks." He crumpled the napkin. "Others have tried and failed to preach me back to the fold."

"That's where they went wrong." She itched to stroke his back in comfort. "I have no intention of preaching at you."

He grunted, scanning the trees, the bushes, everywhere but her and the unconscious Russian.

Her gaze lifted to Lexi. The dog remained standing in the same position. Her partner needed a break.

"We have to tie him up." Natasha motioned to the criminal.

Ian stiffened.

"We can't risk him coming after us." Natasha scanned the downed man. "And we need time to leave the area."

The frown pulling Ian's mouth down deepened.

"Don't worry. His buddies will find him soon enough." She had no doubt the Mafia would hunt for their comrade. She, Ian, and Lexi had to be long gone when that happened. "Can you search him?"

He didn't lift his hands or shift into position.

She started to roll onto her knees. "I'll do it."

Ian grunted, then began diving through the Russian's coat pockets. A satellite phone emerged, along with a pack of cigarettes and a lighter. Moving to the man's pants, Ian came up with nothing. No identification or wallet solidified her belief that the man was a pro. He'd been in the game long enough to know not to carry anything that led to the Mafia. If she was back in Philly, she'd scan the man's fingerprints and possibly find a thick file on the guy, but that wasn't an option. She had nothing to even jerry-rig a way to capture his fingerprints for later processing.

Frustration burned in her lungs. All she could do was take the man's picture and hope the tech wizards back home could come up with a name.

Ian cranked his face toward her. "Problem?"

"No." She groped her thigh, trying to undo the buttons securing the side cargo pocket. Snarling, she pulled on the material, but it refused to thread over the button.

A big hand swatted her fingers away.

Humiliation scorched her cheeks and spread down her throat. She *hated* being helpless. The simplest tasks eluded her now.

In seconds, Ian had both buttons undone.

Natasha couldn't meet his eyes, not that he spared her more than a passing glance. "Thank you," she mumbled. Unable to stand having anyone watch her struggle, she asked, "Can you see if there are strong vines or something we can use as ties?"

Every second they delayed was another second the Russian could wake up.

Ian stood, scanned their surroundings, then marched out of sight.

Natasha managed to pull her phone out of the pocket and powered it on. Not surprising, it couldn't find a cell or data signal. But it could still take pictures. Tucking the phone into her sling, she squirmed, wiggled, and huffed in the most ungraceful performance of standing yet. If anyone at the station ever saw this, they'd never let her live it down. Knowing them, they'd film it and play it during her shifts to some kind of music that made it worse.

Compassionate, they were not.

She loved it.

Once she had her breath back to a reasonable pace, she snapped a few pictures and made sure they saved in her photo gallery. With that done, she noted the time…wow. It was after six already. Powering the phone off to save the battery, she tucked it away. This time, the buttons cooperated. Well, she managed to secure them both with only a few threats and a modicum of teeth-grinding.

Ian returned with his arms full of long vegetation, some still trickling dirt from their roots.

The muscle ticking in his jaw revealed a slew of emotions simmering under the surface. She didn't fault him for the maelstrom. Backed in a corner, fighting for his life, then dealing with the aftermath wasn't easy. She just hoped he didn't add it to his list of reasons to remain angry at her.

That last thought brought her up short. Why did she care

if Ian stayed mad? Her breathing stuttered. Wait. When had Dalton become *Ian*? She already knew the answer. When he'd saved her and Lexi's lives. He hadn't fought for himself. He'd become enraged when the Russian threatened them. Her heart softened and her soul sighed. *Oh no.* This couldn't be happening. She couldn't afford a distraction. She had to remain focused on finding Randy Puckett.

"They'll have to be braided to add strength."

She jolted at the statement ripping her from the unwanted epiphany. "Uh." She cleared her throat. "Can you do it? I don't have both hands."

He dropped the pile by the Russian's boots. "Hold the tops while I weave the stalks together."

Chapter Fourteen

Ian adjusted the second assault rifle clanging against the first on his back. How had his life come to this? His boots crunched over more forest detritus.

He imagined he looked like one of those guerilla-warfare gunslingers with the barrels of both guns rising above his shoulders. Ridiculous.

He kicked a dead branch, but it only broke into pieces instead of launching. That ignited another ember in the rage simmering just below the surface.

He should've said no. His boots stomped a defenseless patch of long grass. Agreeing to fly Natasha Greene and her dog had ruined his life. Okay, the accusation of smuggling and subsequent investigation for the past five months had ruined his life, but this had destroyed the small piece he'd salvaged. His gut had warned him. Tried telling him to run away as far and as fast as he could, but he'd ignored it. It'd whispered she'd change his life forever. If only he'd listened.

But he hadn't. Now he'd lost his plane, his only source of income; had been shot at and hunted by Russian *Mafia*; and there was a possible bomb maker in the area. Incredible. Only a director would believe all this and highlight it in an epic action movie. While he could never replace the Cessna sentimentally, he could eventually buy another plane. In theory, he could also outrun the Mafia, but what he couldn't digest was learning he had an animal side. Natasha had forced him—fine, the Russian threatening to *kill* her and Lexi forced him—into a situation where he had to tap into a savagery he'd never known existed. But he'd never have discovered that side of him if *Officer Greene* had been honest from the start. *Maybe.* He kicked a small rock. *Be honest.* He probably would've accepted the fare because he needed the money to fight the investigation. At least he would've been better prepared.

He barely remembered anything after he picked up the branch. The ferocity overtook him completely. All reasoning and humanity had disappeared…

He swallowed the bile rising in his throat. If he hadn't heard Natasha shout, he'd have seriously hurt that man. Kept swinging the branch—

Veering to the right, he disappeared between two trees. Crouching, dry heaves plagued his stomach and killed his ribs. *Ugh.*

Lexi wormed next to him in the branches. She placed her jaw on his forearm as if to offer comfort.

Against his will, he softened. Staring into her big brown eyes, he felt her support and understanding.

"Dalton?"

Ian wiped his wet eyes on his coat sleeves. Natasha had let him tromp ahead, obviously sensing his need to be alone to deal with his temper and confusion. Now she'd caught up.

Lexi trotted away and he gritted his teeth as he stood. His ribs let him know they didn't appreciate the jostling. The last thing he wanted Natasha to see was him losing his stomach again. Once in front of her was bad enough. The woman was the epitome of tough and courageous. As conflicted as he was about her, he couldn't deny that.

He needed to take a page out of her book, even if he had to bluff.

As he trekked closer, Natasha's dark hazel irises surrounded by bruises studied him. She didn't say a word as they fell in step together. He had the urge to thank her for remaining quiet but didn't want to break the silence. His thoughts were still too jumbled and his emotions refused to settle.

The rifles on his back clattered together, the sound jarring in the quiet density of the forest.

Mafia Two hadn't had any spare magazines for the automatic rifle... Ian's jaw tightened. Spare magazines? Until today, he couldn't tell a magazine from a clip. Ask him about lumber or the best way to frame a room and he'd go on for hours. Weaponry? He floundered. Though his real passion was being in the air. Flying. Being free to soar. Cruising the open skies. No investigations or other worries touched him when he left the runway.

"We *have* to find the hideout," Natasha stated for the second time, the first lobbed at him before he trudged ahead of her earlier.

He ignored it again. His main goal was to find shelter, then food and water. He refused to entertain a conversation that didn't matter. Survival basics topped the list. Bomb makers and Russians fell to the bottom.

Hopefully, they stayed there. As much as he wanted to avoid the criminals, they had confiscated everything; Ian's gear and hunting rifle, Natasha's luggage and satellite phone. Why she insisted on reclaiming her phone when they had two now, he hadn't taken the time to find out.

"Ian," Natasha snapped. "I know you can hear me."

Everything in a quarter-mile radius could hear her. He might be roped into helping her, but that didn't mean he had to mindlessly follow everything she said. Her priorities were not his. She needed him to navigate the forest and take charge of survival, and he planned to do just that.

"Ace."

Something smacked the side of his head.

He halted, glaring at the woman who topped out at his mouth. "Did you just hit me?"

"Nope." She plucked a pinecone off a white spruce and tossed it at his chest. The brown cone bounced off his coat and thudded into the dirt.

He stared at it, then lifted his gaze. "Seriously?"

"I had to get your attention somehow." She jabbed a finger at him. "You've done an amazing job ignoring me."

His gaze lifted to the sky. The clouds had grown thicker, darker, and the temperature had dropped another few degrees. Wind gusts blew stronger and more often, and now that he paid attention, small animals had become scarce. Foreboding curled in his gut.

"We have to find the hideout."

And that made number three.

"I heard you the first two times." He braced his hands on his hips, then moved his right hand. He didn't want to highlight the revolver holstered beneath his coat. If she hadn't mentioned it by now, he figured she probably hadn't seen him pull it out on the first Mafia criminal. Of the two of them, she was more qualified to handle it, but he was reluctant to give it up. With it on his hip, he cut the casualties to zero. If she held it, she might use it.

"Could've fooled me," she muttered, scowling at him. "We have to catch the bomb maker before he escapes."

"No," he countered. "We have to find shelter before we tangle with a bomb maker and his Mafia friends." A statement he never thought he'd utter.

"I *have* to learn his plans," she growled, frustration creasing the space between her brows. "He's planning something big. I *have* to find out what it is. I need to stop it or at least send out a warning."

That made him bite back the snarl ready to fly past his lips. He couldn't argue with stopping a bomb, but… He pointed at the sky. "See those clouds? They're building into something nasty. If we don't find shelter soon, we're going to be in trouble."

"And if we don't find their hideout, we'll miss them clearing out," she shot back.

"They aren't leaving in the next few hours."

"You don't know that." She jutted her chin. "Randy Puckett could feel he's been compromised."

Unable to think of a comeback, he switched tactics. "Did you *try* to use the Russian's phones?" Ian pointed at her sling. "What was the point of taking them? You should've called for rescue by now."

"We only have one." Her chin lifted.

"We have *two*." He held up two fingers to emphasize the point. "You made me search *both* men." Violating their privacy still gave him the willies.

"I lost one when you flung me into the bushes." Dark hazel eyes heated with her glare. "Thanks for that, by the way. It didn't hurt *at all*."

"My foot dropped into a *hole*," he retorted. "You tried to catch me. *Physics* did the rest." He pointed at the sling again. "You haven't tried the one?"

"We've been a little busy and I only have one hand." She fished out a black device the length of his hand, sporting a thick antenna on the top. Similar to a regular cell phone, it had a small screen above a keypad with green and red buttons for sending and ending calls. The outer shell looked military-grade and like it could withstand a war.

Natasha fumbled with it in her palm until she hit the green button with her thumb. Bold black type across the screen read "Password" with a space below to enter the combination.

"It's locked." She tapped on the keypad with no success. "*Of course* it's locked. It won't even allow 9-1-1 calls." She growled. "Nothing's been easy."

He hung his head and exhaled. Searching those men had been for *nothing*. Hope shattered into impotence. They still had no way to call for help. Their only avenue resided inside a Mafia-controlled hideout.

A hale of wind grabbed the brim of his hat, trying to rip it off. He smacked a hand on his head, saving it. Dread coiled in his gut, whispering they didn't have much time before the brewing storm hit.

Natasha readjusted her hat, then drew back her arm and threw the phone.

His jaw dropped as he gaped at the black device disappearing in the trees. "Why did you do that?" It wasn't a shout, but it was close. Sure, the phone was useless, but...

"GPS." Quick breaths resounded through her lungs and her skin paled as she hugged herself. "I didn't think about it until this second." She scowled at him, correctly reading he was about to comment. "Blame the broken bones, damaged lungs, or pounding headache."

He snapped his lips closed, unwilling to admit his own head hammered with the concussion, not to mention his squealing ribs. She had to be downright *miserable*.

"I researched a lot before I bought mine," she continued, clueless about his silent sympathy. "Most have locators in the phones. I doubt the Russians turned them off. They probably figured they could use it to find lost comrades in the wilderness."

Blood drained from his head and he swayed. His concussed brain hadn't thought about GPS locators. Now he obsessed about them. They hadn't escaped. The Mafia probably followed their progress. They could be creeping closer as he stood arguing with the infuriating woman.

He pivoted.

"Wait," Natasha shouted.

Another thump smacked the back of his head. His fingers curled into fists. If she hit him with a pinecone one more time… "I'm not sticking around to greet your buddies."

"They're *not* my *buddies*," she puffed, doing nothing to squelch her stomps through the forest. "We have to head toward the plane. The hideout is somewhere close. I'd say less than a mile by how fast the Russians came the second time around."

"And walk straight into the next felon itching to put a bullet in my head? No thanks."

Lexi trotted up next to him, then kept pace.

His fingers scratched between her ears as if drawn by an unknown force. The short black fur comforted his nerves.

"Ian, I'm serious—"

"So am I, *Nat*," he tossed over his shoulder.

"Where are you going?" Her wheezing deepened.

He jabbed forward. It was as good of a direction as any and he hoped to find something he could use to make a shelter. Without an axe, he didn't have much chance.

Boot thumps stopped. "Fine, *Ace*. You do your thing." Something skittered into the trees. He imagined a dead branch toppling end over end. "I'm going to find that hideout."

Ian rounded a towering white spruce. He was calling her bluff. He'd watch from behind the tree and wait for her to come to her senses. Once she realized he was right, he could search in peace.

Chapter Fifteen

Natasha fought with the cargo pocket buttons again. Next time she ordered tactical pants for work, she was getting Velcro. She didn't care if it made a ripping sound and gave her position away, buttons were the bane of her existence.

Lexi stopped in front of Natasha and sat, her tongue lolling out the side.

"Enjoying the show?" Natasha muttered. Wind smacked against her back, pushing her forward.

Lexi bolted up as Natasha took a balancing step.

Eyeing the darkening sky, she bit her lip. "Maybe Ian's right."

Lexi peered his way, but he had already disappeared among the trees.

"Well." Natasha snapped her shoulders back. "So am I."

With a grin of triumph, she freed one of the buttons. Worming her hand inside, she pulled out her cell phone. Powering it on, she tapped the surface until a large compass filled the screen.

Ha! She beamed, twisting her body with the phone held flat in front. She had paid for a version that didn't require the internet, and it *worked*. With every movement, the directional indicator turned with her. As a bonus, the app didn't use much energy. Battery-saving score.

She glanced at the surrounding trees. Her jubilation faded. One problem. She hadn't noted the direction of the plane when they fled. In all the upheaval, she forgot about the app.

Dropping her arm, she blew out a breath. If her head would stop pounding for five minutes, she could come up with a plan.

Lexi yawned.

Natasha was right there with her. She wanted a nap. And water. Food. Definitely a shower, and a pain pill…

This wasn't helping.

Studying her partner, Natasha wondered if Lexi could find the plane. The dog usually had something to scent before she searched, but maybe if their circumstances were extreme enough, Lexi would understand. Though, asking her to find a plane went beyond anything they'd ever tried before. Natasha inwardly shrugged. She had to try.

"Lexi."

The German shepherd perked up, her brown eyes intent on Natasha.

"Seek plane," Natasha commanded, signing the directive.

Lexi cocked her head, her tail beginning to wag.

"You want to find a plane?" Natasha asked, her voice filled with enthusiasm.

Lexi stood, her head searching.

"Find the plane, girl." She ramped up her enthusiasm to excite her partner. "Seek."

Lexi started trotting.

Early in their training, Natasha and Lexi had found a mutual pace. In the beginning, the dog used to take off, leaving Natasha in the dust, but no longer. Only if Natasha added "fast" to the command did the dog run.

Natasha blinked at the direction.

"Lexi?"

The dog paused and looked over her shoulder.

"Seek *plane*," Natasha repeated.

The dog faced forward and limped ahead again.

"Where are you going?" Natasha shoved her phone into her sling and trudged after her partner.

Thirty feet ahead, Lexi veered to the right and disappeared behind a tree.

Natasha did her best to avoid the dead twigs and branches trying to trip her.

Lexi reappeared, then lay on her belly. The signal she'd found something.

"If you're leading me to a bunny, I'm not giving you your chew toy."

Natasha strongly believed in positive reinforcement; a reward instead of punishment. As part of K-9 training from the time Lexi was a puppy, whenever she performed her task correctly, she got to play with a toy. Her favorite was a cross-eyed crocodile on the end of a thick rope. No idea why, but Natasha bought a case of them so she was prepared if the manufacturer ever discontinued the line.

Natasha finally reached the dog, who now stood and rounded the tree.

"Ruff. Ruff."

Natasha halted at the happy yips. Why was she—

Lexi reappeared as footsteps thumped.

Adrenaline surged along with confusion. Lexi—

"Give up already?"

Natasha's gaze snapped to the man waltzing into view. "Ace."

"Nat." He stopped a few feet away. "Now we can—"

"He's *not* the plane." Natasha pointed at Ian but stared at her partner.

Lexi cocked her head. She then looked between Ian and Natasha.

"Plane," Natasha stubbornly repeated and signed.

The dog nudged Ian's thigh with her nose.

"You expected the dog to find the Cessna?" Ian rocked back on his heels.

"I need the direction." Natasha snatched her phone out and held it up to the stubborn pilot. The compass needle bounced. "Randy Puckett can't escape."

"Nat." Ian motioned to the ominous sky. "*We* might not survive the storm."

"All the more reason to find the hideout."

"Alaska doesn't have hurricanes like you're used to on the East Coast." His grim expression underlined his warning. "It's much worse here. The storms that strike are massive, blowing in from the Bering Sea." He spread his arms. "A lot of times they cover most of the state."

Terrifying. Now she *really* had to convince him to help her. It might already be too late. "Randy is responsible for so much worse than what he did to us." She motioned to herself, then at Lexi. "He's planning another attack. Something big. More explosions are going to hurt and kill innocent people."

"Natasha." His frown deepened.

"You know I'm right. Ian, please." She'd never begged in her life. "If that doesn't sway you, help me find it so we can recover my satellite phone."

The clock ticking inside urged her to start moving.

He stiffened. "That's not fair."

"None of this is fair."

He eyed the darkening sky again.

"He's set up somewhere near the crash," she pressed. She was losing to his instinct to protect them from the storm. The replay of the Russians popping over the steep hill filled her mind. "Once we're at the plane, I'll know which direction to head."

He crossed his arms.

"But I have to find the Cessna first."

The muscle in his jaw ticked.

She straightened. "You know which way to go." Something about the way he reacted nudged her instincts. "Tell me."

He stared at her for too many seconds. "Ian?" She placed her hand on his coat sleeve, meeting his conflicted pale green eyes. "Please take us back to the plane."

Marching back toward the Cessna, Ian inwardly groaned at his capitulation. Big hazel eyes begging him to help was apparently his Achilles' heel. The bruises on her face, the sling holding broken bones, and the wheeze emanating from her lungs chipped at the last vestiges of anger harboring in his heart. She had tried to argue that he knew she was right. He didn't know any such thing except that this woman did not beg. It was obvious from the flit of surprise in her pleading expression that she hadn't meant to. That small revelation of honesty sliced through his determination to win the latest battle of wills.

Ian? Please take us back to the plane. Her words curled around his heart. Not Dalton, but *Ian.* She'd said his first name before, but now it was different. Another shift had happened. One he wasn't prepared for. Using his first name shattered the distance. It invited warmth and acceptance, telling him she saw him as a man, not just the pilot.

Some part of her had been comfortable enough to beg for his help.

Giddiness stole through him at the realization while the rest of him wanted to smack some sense into his head. Now that he didn't face her, pessimistic thoughts whispered in his mind. Barreling into danger was not in his job description. Well, if he didn't count bush piloting. That was nothing but danger, but willfully walking *toward* the Mafia was extreme. The Russians could already be in the area thanks to the GPS in the satellite phone. Did that deter Officer Natasha Greene?

Nope. The woman had an oversize dose of valor. Or an all-consuming vengeance disguised as justice.

Tree branches clacked together as leaves whipped and swirled past.

A shiver stole down his spine and he hunched against the bluster. She believed she had won this round, but really it was a draw. No, he didn't want to hide where the Russians could find them, *but* he realized his plane was their saving grace. They could use it to ride out the storm. He didn't need an axe to enclose the three of them into something relatively safe from the elements.

Slowing their pace, he carefully edged around a prickly rosebush and ferns. The same ones as before. Even though the area had them in abundance, this set was missing flower petals from Natasha's crash landing.

The hairs along the back of his neck stood and he peeked between a spruce's branches.

"We close?" Natasha whispered against his shoulder.

Lexi sniffed the ground.

"Not to the plane." He continued to search. "I'm sure this is the spot where we tied up the Russian, but I don't see anyone."

Natasha peered around the tree. "His comrades found him, I guess."

Ian's shoulders slumped. A heavy weight lifted and he inhaled a complete breath. He hadn't realized how much the man's survival weighed on him.

Dismay played over her face. "That means their hideout is filled with angry, injured Russians."

His stomach plunged. He hadn't thought of it that way.

"We *have* to find them." Natasha strode forward. "We can't wait. This could be the catalyst that has them abandoning the hideout."

Her anxious worry rubbed off on him. Without another word, he motioned for her to go first. It wasn't chivalry but caution that had him trailing behind. MT might've vanished, but Ian kept imagining another Mafia killer lurking in the area.

Chapter Sixteen

Randy set the soldering tool into a makeshift cradle, and sat back in the metal folding chair. The magnifying glass secured to the table amplified the intricate workings of the fail-safe he built into every bomb.

The single spotlight on the other side of the table gave him a headache. The harsh light was too bright and garish, causing deep shadows beyond its reach. But he didn't bother with additional lighting. They had two gas generators in soundproof boxes. One for his workspace, the other for the living area to run essentials. With only a few gas cans left, they conserved as much as possible.

Not that he cared anymore.

The urgency to escape Alaska rode him hard. His imagination kept coughing up scenarios of the FBI and police storming in. The safety measures he'd stashed around the building only went so far. He may kill a few officers, but another wave could overwhelm the traps. The last phase of the revolution's prep rested on his shoulders. He *had* to remain free.

"Plane no coming," Pasha announced, barreling into the clean room, the plastic flaps fluttering behind him.

Randy jumped to his feet. "Why?"

"Weather bad." Pasha strode to the table and frowned at the device beneath the magnifying glass. "You no finish."

Randy ground his teeth. He wanted that plane on the ground, ready to go the second he completed the job. It took the threat of not working another second before Pasha called his boss to arrange the flight with Randy's payment in the cargo hold. Now he had no way to escape.

"Work." Pasha pointed at the bomb.

The muscle in Randy's jaw ticked. The Russians refused to let him leave until he completed their order. They didn't care if the plane wreck meant discovery. They had too much faith in their automatic rifles to play it smart.

He was supposed to be the authority in this venture, but Pasha had mutinied when Pyotr stopped communicating. The Mafia leader used his weapon to enforce his will on Randy. The only concession Randy had managed was the plane arriving early.

A commotion in the other room saved Randy from saying something he shouldn't.

Following Pasha into the main area, he found Andrei struggling to lay Pyotr on an air mattress beside Vanya's. Russian language flew between Pasha, Andrei, and Pyotr. Vanya was currently passed out.

"What happened?" Randy demanded, hating not understanding a word.

Andrei sat on the edge of the mattress. "Pyotr find man, woman, dog."

Pyotr groaned, his hand moving to the back of his head. "Man knock me out."

"Tied him." Andrei pulled a wad of plants out of his pocket.

Randy blinked at the remains of braided vegetation.

"Find Vanya phone near Pyotr." Andrei plucked the satellite device from a different pocket.

Another round of Russian conversation had Andrei shaking his head. "No."

Pasha grimaced. "They take Pyotr weapon too."

The knot in Randy's stomach tightened. The man and woman had enough presence of mind to take the satellite phones and guns, but they didn't have basic supplies like rope or handcuffs. An inkling of who the bush pilot had chartered formed in his mind. His gaze drifted to the haphazard pile stacked in the corner. It was time to go through the items confiscated from the plane.

Randy marched to the jumbled stack. "I'm searching this." He grabbed a red backpack. "I suggest you send Andrei back out. They've probably tried to use Pyotr's phone by now." With no success. Even if they had the password, Randy would've received an alert on his computer that the phone was in use. "Maybe they don't know we can track it."

Thunder cracked overhead.

Natasha jolted at the echoing boom.

The tops of the towering spruces swayed, their branches smacking together wildly in the constant wind.

Dark gray clouds covered the sky, sending goose bumps all over her skin. Ominous creaking ratcheted her nerves and she prayed the tree trunks withstood the harrowing gusts.

She'd experienced thunderstorms before, but none that looked or felt like this.

"We have to hurry," Ian shouted from behind.

The wind snatched his words to the point she barely heard him.

Natasha smashed her left hand on her hat to keep it on her head. Clinging to her phone with her right hand and using the sling to keep it anchored, she glanced at the compass dial. The directional arrow hadn't moved much, unlike the howling wind.

Lexi bowed her head, fighting to push forward.

"Nat," Ian yelled.

She clenched her teeth. He'd been warned she didn't answer to the abbreviation. Okay, she did on occasion, but earlier they'd been locked in a battle of wills. Now... If she didn't respond he'd get the hint. Maybe.

There. She peeked at the dial again to orient the landmark. The stream flowing between the two steep hills curved in front of her. If she followed it, she'd find the plane.

But what if...

She studied her surroundings. The trees had thinned, spacing farther apart. They were getting closer to the clearing surrounding the wreck. Unfortunately, that meant shrubs, bushes, and other plants flourished, many taller than her.

Another crack of thunder made her jump.

"Natasha Greene," Ian bellowed. "I know you can hear me."

With the wind gusting, she almost couldn't. Now he knew what she felt like when he ignored her.

Lexi struggled to find footing among the spreading berry bushes.

Natasha wheezed, her damaged lungs feeling as if a fire burned within. The rough terrain had been ascending, forming the steep hills she hoped to avoid.

"Stop." A large hand clamped on to her left bicep.

She snapped her gaze to Ian's. "Let go. I think I've found an easier way to the hideout."

"We have to take shelter in the plane." The creases in his face deepened as he glanced at the scary sky.

"Let me see if I'm right."

"No." His hold tightened. "We'll investigate once this storm passes."

She didn't have time to wait. A clock ticked loudly in

her head. The window to catch the bomb maker was closing, but her instincts warned that Ian wouldn't care.

So she'd go on without him.

Natasha relaxed her stance and nodded. "Fine. But you lead the way."

His eyes narrowed.

"You're bigger." She jutted her chin at his body. "You can make a path for me." Not really a selling point, seeing as they were trying *not* to leave a trail.

He held on for a few more breath-holding seconds, then let go and tromped forward.

Natasha flashed a hand signal to Lexi to stay by Natasha's side.

The dog moved to stand on Natasha's left.

The wind howled, bending the shrubs to alarming angles. Chills skittered over her skin, but she ignored them. If she didn't find that hideout, she'd lose Randy Puckett.

Not happening. He wouldn't get away this time.

Chapter Seventeen

Natasha's boot slipped and splashed into the water.

"Yieeee," she yelped, then snapped her mouth closed, fervently checking to see if Ian had heard the cry. The skin and muscles above her boot rippled at the frigid water soaking her pants.

Shivering with her heart in her throat, she spied snatches of Ian's tan coat peeking through the swaying vegetation. She exhaled. He continued at a steady pace, not alarmed in the least.

The stream was only a few feet wide in this section and she planned to take advantage.

Let's go, let's go, let's go. Utilizing stones and debris, she stumbled through the stream as fast as possible.

Lexi jumped, landing on three legs, avoiding the water altogether.

"Show-off," Natasha grumbled, jealous she couldn't do the same.

Wind pounded against her face and chest, driving her backward, but she persevered and made it to the other side.

Thunder boomed, rumbling across the sky.

Startled, the ball of her foot landed on a rock that twisted. She lost her balance just as the skies opened. Freezing rain struck her, knocking her to the ground. Air flew from her lungs as a sharp pain radiated up her spine from falling on her tailbone.

White lights blinked in her sight and it took three tries to inhale. Pellets beat against her head, bouncing off her hat and trying to burrow into her clothing.

"Get up," she muttered the command.

Lexi hunched next to Natasha, her large head bowed against the onslaught.

Gale winds were surging harder than before.

"We can't quit." She kissed the dog's snout, smacking her lips at the wet fur coating her lips. "We'll get him this time."

Vow reiterated, Natasha steeled herself to stand. Without Ian to pull her up, she resorted to rolling on her side and kneeling.

Something hard crunched under her knee.

Yeow. She slid to the side.

"Oh no." A jagged crack slithered across the screen of her cell phone lying in fast-forming mud. She snatched her phone out of the puddle and rubbed it on her wet pants.

Please work. She willed the device to listen. The compass still showed on the screen, though the directional arrow winked in and out. Twisting with the phone, the arrow froze, then finally adjusted.

Good enough. She shoved it back into her sling to protect it from the rain and awkwardly rose to her feet.

The sleet-mix downpour overwhelmed her jacket's water-resistant material. It plastered to her body, trapping in the cold.

This latest round of misery was a trial she'd overcome.

Water rolling off the brim of her cap further complicated her study of the terrain. From what she could make out, the ground continued ascending at a steady degree but wasn't as steep as the hills near the plane.

It was better than nothing.

Splashing accompanied every step, sloshing icy water inside her boots. Her poor toes were frozen. The sleet had no mercy.

She forged ahead, her body angled forward to combat the wind.

She couldn't give up. *Wouldn't* give up until Randy Puckett was behind bars. For life.

Ian's gaze bounced wildly, unable to settle.

He'd lost Natasha. Lost Lexi. How could he lose a pair who had trouble walking?

Mud splattered up his jeans and the wet denim chaffed his skin. His steel-toed boots kept his feet relatively dry, but he had nothing to protect his hands.

His hood kept losing the battle to the wind. He put it up, the wind knocked it back. Zipping his coat to the top helped, but his frozen fingers fumbled with the strings on each side to tighten the hood.

He didn't have time for this. Letting go, he growled, still incapable of focusing his attention.

The merciless sleet pounded the ground, obscuring his ability to see beyond a few feet.

Vindictive whispers told him to forget Natasha and finish finding the plane. He'd be safe and warm—ish? Well, out of the hurricane-type wind and freezing rain.

His conscience muzzled the spiteful thoughts and locked them in a dark hole. If this had happened right after the crash, he might've listened. Now…now he *had* to find her. The infuriating woman had burrowed beneath his skin. He'd never met a more obstinate, willful, hard-headed, courageous, loyal, amazing woman. She didn't fit into his life. In fact, she was a complication, no, heartache waiting to happen. If she ever found out about the investigation, she'd leave him flat. Yet, his heart pounded against his chest, frantic to locate her.

Sleet smacked against the brim of his hat, bouncing off at dizzying speeds. Swiping his thumb across the compass swiveling on his watch, he squinted at the direction. Where was he? He twisted, his wild gaze not settling enough to help.

Please be okay, he prayed. God had deserted him, but maybe He'd listen to a plea since it was for Natasha and Lexi.

Thunder cracked, then rolled.

His lizard brain pumped signals to hide, find shelter, escape. Curling a fist, he fought to override the basic instincts.

Move. His boots slopped in the mud, destroying berry bushes and weeds.

The deepening stream cutting through the clearing frothed and beat against the rock bed. Somewhere close ahead, his plane lay in pieces against a black spruce.

Wrong way. The Russians didn't run from the direction of the stream. He quarter-turned, jamming his heels into the angled ground. He only made it a few steps when the loam gave way. Throwing his hand out, he latched on to a Scouler's willow arched over in the wind. The branches creaked and bent, but kept him from sliding into the ravine on his stomach.

He used the shrubs to walk up the steep hill, like a rock climber used rope. Once he ran out of branches, he scrabbled to hold on to anything he could to keep moving upward.

Sourness coated his tongue, fear bitter in his mouth. What if she was hurt? What if she had fallen and couldn't move? Would Lexi be able to find him? What if Lexi was hurt and Natasha couldn't find him to help?

Questions continued to plague his mind, clogging his ability to think. He couldn't allow himself to want a relationship, but he wasn't ready to let her go yet. He'd barely learned a thing about her. What caused her injuries? Why had she become a police officer? What was her favorite color?

When his hands couldn't latch on to anything else he realized he'd made it to the top. Gale winds blasted against him, forcing him to lean forward or fall backward. The stream valley below had filtered the impact. Now he experienced the full brunt.

Snapping his arm up, he protected his eyes from flying dirt and debris. Twigs and dead branches cartwheeled past, dropping over the edge.

The guns on his back clanged together as if rattling a warning. He wanted to toss them into the wind but didn't. He may hate the violence they represented, but he wasn't about to give up the protection.

Putting one foot in front of the other took every ounce of strength. Hunching his shoulders, he struggled to keep moving forward. The drive to find Natasha drummed harder in his veins. She had put her life on the line for him; he needed to return the favor. His life wasn't worth more than hers. In fact, she had way more value. All he did lately was hide in Alaska. The ridiculous investigation would eventually end, and he had nothing to return to. His job wouldn't accept him back, and he wanted nothing to do with his ex-fiancée. She'd left him the moment he told her about the accusation. She didn't care about his innocence, only that the scandal touched her.

For the past five months, he'd been existing, not living. Natasha and Lexi had shown him the difference. He no longer bore any anger at Officer Greene. Yes, she withheld vital facts that led to the loss of his Cessna, but he wasn't entirely innocent. She was right, he could've landed in a different spot or not at all. As the pilot, *he* made the final decisions regarding the plane, not the passenger.

A twig full of green leaves whapped his chest, then slid across his coat to sail in the wind again.

The sleet and debris made it impossible to see. How was he going to find her?

"Lexi," he bellowed. Maybe the dog's superior hearing could help him.

Quiet, his fear scolded. *Don't shout.* The Mafia killers could be anywhere. The last thing he wanted was to stumble into the path of their assault rifles. At some point, he had to come to terms with the terror and savagery the criminals invoked. But now he knew he had the ability to confront evil, not cower. Natasha had been defenseless when MT threatened her. Not that he saw her as helpless. Even with all her injuries, he never considered her weak. Her personality and determination dared anyone to see her as anything less than strong and courageous.

And he didn't...just foolish. Her drive to catch the bomb maker had gone from valiant to obsession.

He paused. Cocking his head, he strained to hear over the blasts of wind. He couldn't decipher anything.

"Lexi," he bellowed again. He swore he heard a bark.

Two lumbering steps later, he stopped. The deep-throated bark of the dog carried on a gust.

Chapter Eighteen

"Where are you going?" Natasha cried, reaching out like that would stop her dog from sprinting away. "Lexi."

The dog disappeared in the wall of sleet and rain.

Natasha hunched over, gasping, unable to suck in enough air. With the wind constantly barreling past, it should've been easy to inhale oxygen, but she couldn't. Her lungs burned and she coughed into her frozen palm.

Bright red skin warned of potential frostbite and she growled. It was *August*. Alaska was part of the United States. She hadn't traveled to Antarctica.

True, but she'd traveled close to the Arctic Circle.

Grumbling at the smarty-pants answer her logic provided, she managed to force her fingers to curl. They hurt. The sleet kept driving its iciness into her skin.

Against her lungs' protest, she pushed against the barrier of air trying to knock her back.

Somewhere ahead, the forest began. She remembered from their circling in the plane, the clearing ranged about a half mile in all directions with the stream at the center. She just had to make it to the trees. Hopefully, they'd block most of the wind and rain—

"*Woof. Woof. Woof.*"

Natasha snapped her head toward the faint barking. "Lexi?"

Nothing but sleet greeted her sight. Biting her raw lip, Natasha debated if she should wait or continue. Her labored breathing begged for a rest, but the urgency singing in her blood demanded she keep moving.

Coughing, she staggered another step. Lexi could find her—

The German shepherd appeared like an apparition though the cascade of falling water.

Before she could scold the dog for running off, Ian emerged.

"Nat, stop."

"No." She twisted, rushing to escape his reaching hand. "Don't touch me." The words tore at her abused lungs. "I'm finding that hideout."

"You have to stop." Ian's long stride caught up to her too easily. He jumped into her path, obstructing her progress. "It's too dangerous."

Gale winds howled as another boom of thunder rolled.

"I can't," she yelled, wincing at her throat burning along with everything else. She stepped to the side. "He can't escape—"

"Listen to yourself," he shouted, the wind obscuring his words. "You're obsessed."

"Of course I am," she barked, unable to look into his face. Too much flying debris and particles had her slitting her eyes. "He—" A choked sob came out of nowhere.

"Nat." Ian crowded closer.

"No." She fought against the lump in her throat. She hadn't cried since the first day she woke up in the hospital and found out Lexi was going to be okay. She was *not* going to break down now.

"You're not thinking." His hand cradled her left shoulder.

"I *have* to find him." Another sob ripped free. "I

have…" She couldn't squeeze the words past the lump in her throat.

Unbidden, her left knee buckled and she toppled. Mud and water splattered her pants and jacket. Bending forward, she screamed, but no sound came out.

"Why?"

She opened her eyes to find Ian on the ground beside her, the weight of his heavy hand only now registering on her back.

"Why is it so important?" he asked gruffly against her ear. "I get he should be caught—"

"Lexi almost *died*," she croaked, grabbing the front of his jacket and squeezing. "Because I *failed*. I failed to find him in time, then he tried to kill us." As it was, he succeeded in murdering three innocent people, and injuring dozens of others in the Liberty Bell explosion.

She hoarsely screamed to free the anger, terror, and pain.

Ian wrapped his body around the weeping woman as best he could without hurting her.

Never had he felt so inadequate in his life.

Abject grief radiated off the broken woman, triggering tears in the corners of his eyes. The howling winds, driving rain, and raging thunder were nothing compared to the maelstrom in his arms.

"How?" He cleared his throat and tried again. "What happened?"

Her body wracked with barely audible sobs.

He shifted to take the brunt of her weight, maneuvering her head to rest on his chest and shoulder. Her hat tried to get in the way, but he adjusted it.

Lexi whined, crowding his other side. She sat and placed her paw on his thigh as she leaned forward to lick Natasha's cheek.

Natasha didn't seem to register the affection.

How long had it been since she allowed herself to feel the sorrow? Judging by the way she clung to him, he bet she hadn't dealt with the tragedy at all. Not that he was one to judge. He treated emotions like the plague.

Resting his cheek on top of her drenched and *cold* hat, he rubbed her spine. Wind pounded against his back and he hoped they could still escape harm from the storm. He had to get her to safety.

"Randy Puckett."

She spoke into his coat. Between the storm and her position, he had trouble hearing.

She'd said the name before, but only now did he pay attention. Ian had been in Alaska when Randy made the news, but it was hard to forget a bombing in America. "Didn't he try to blow up the Liberty Bell?"

"Yes." Another round of sobs wracked her body. "We knew…something was…coming."

He curled his frozen fingers around the back of her neck.

"Ian." Her left fist thumped the back of his coat. "I failed."

"You—"

"No," she cut in. "Lexi's trained for explosive detection and searches." Natasha beat his coat again. "But she needs *me* to give her a place to start." Another sob tore from her throat. "I didn't find him until after it was too late to save those people."

Shame strangled Natasha's voice. Memories of that day played in her mind in vivid, ultrasound HD. If she confessed her failure, he'd understand why she *had* to stop Randy from escaping.

"Tourists had taken advantage of the beautiful summer weather that day to visit the famous landmarks downtown." Setting the scene helped ease her into the nightmare. "Independence Hall, the Liberty Bell, museums, and so much more are within walking distance of each other.

"Lexi and I—" she wheezed into Ian's coat "—we had been assigned to scout the area." Her throat tightened. "Rumors of a bomb had been raging for days, but no one could find it."

His arms twinged, hugging her tighter.

"I can still picture the scene vividly." Her memory paused on the site. "Lush trees and freshly mowed grass filled the spaces between bricked walking paths in the dedicated park near the bell." Phantom remnants of the scents blocked the storm's odors. "Crowds of tourists roamed, some carrying maps, others snacks and drinks, all laughing and happy.

"Lexi signaled for me to let her lead." Natasha's palm pulsed as if her partner pulled on a leash again. "I let her take over. She led me to one of the main streets, her nose alternating between the ground and air."

Ian bent closer. "Nat?"

She hadn't realized she'd stopped talking, too busy reliving it. "I didn't know until after the bomb exploded that Lexi scented the device inside a backpack." She inhaled, then exhaled. "It had detonated early, killing three people and injuring dozens more, including the man attempting to place it close to the exhibit."

Her hand gripped the back of his coat. "We didn't find out the target was the Liberty Bell until later."

"You couldn't have known," Ian soothed against her head.

Wind tore at her and rain lashed her exposed skin. It was everything she deserved. "In the chaos, Lexi signaled again."

The video in her head sped up. "I spied Randy Puckett standing on the corner, a block down. The second he noticed me, he ran. Lexi and I chased him on foot. I radi-

oed in, but it didn't do any good. Everyone was respond-
ing to the bombing.

"He ducked into the lobby of a multistory building and
I followed." Her throat seized.

"What happened?" A coarse finger scraped under her
chin as he gently forced her face up. Pale green eyes filled
with unshed tears met hers.

"He set a trap," she managed to push out. "Lexi almost died."

"So did you."

Natasha blinked at the blunt response. No one outside
her mandated therapist had been so candid. "The second
we stepped inside the vestibule, pink foam shot out of a
row of cleverly hidden nozzles anchored on the right. Filling up the space fast. Before I could do more than try to
shelter Lexi, the foam began to expand and harden."

Her ribs and arm screamed as if it happened all over
again. She cried out, gagging at the agony ripping through
her again. The raging storm dropped away and all she saw
and felt was that moment.

Can't breathe. Her lungs wailed for air. The foam
squeezed her like an unrelenting vise.

Air! She couldn't move. All she could see was pink.

Lexi squealed and yelped.

Lexi. Natasha couldn't expand her lungs to talk. *NO!*

Foam sucked into her nose and filled her mouth, suffocating her, burning her throat and lungs. She couldn't
cough. She couldn't move. She couldn't breathe.

The pressure on her body worsened, the pink endlessly
expanding and hardening. Foot by foot, inch by inch, it
squeezed, insisting on crushing her to utilize the space.

I'm going to die. I've killed my partner.

Chapter Nineteen

❧

"*Nat,*" Ian yelled, cupping both her cheeks.

Panic seized his body. *Why won't she respond?* He had to snap her out of the flashback.

"Look at me," he tried again, tightening his grip. "You're not there. You hear me? *You're not in that vestibule.*"

Her eyes remained glassy and filled with so much horror.

He never wanted to see that expression again. The utter terror and conviction of death.

Lexi barked, pawing Natasha's thigh.

Natasha's mouth dropped open in a silent scream. She still lived inside the memory.

Thunder pealed overhead.

The spruces nearby bashed together, the wind roaring harder.

Natasha's lungs hadn't moved since she dropped into the memory. If he didn't get her to breathe, she'd suffocate.

"*Listen to me,*" he bellowed, his nose centimeters from hers.

Nothing.

Hysteria ruled his mind. She *had* to inhale.

Sleet swirled like a blanket in a vigorous wash cycle. Through the wall of rain, a large dead limb hurdled into view.

No! He tucked Natasha's head against his throat and protected her as best he could. "Lexi—"

The dog was already midjump over it.

The branch sailed behind him, twigs stripped of leaves scraping his back as it passed.

Too close. Heart thundering as loud as the storm, he cupped Natasha's face again. They had to find shelter. Winds this vicious ripped trees out of the ground.

But first, Natasha had to breathe. Only one thought popped into his chaotic mind and he went with it. Fitting his mouth over hers, he blew. Twice he gave her oxygen. Should he pump her chest?

Lexi howled, pawing at his coat, demanding he fix her owner.

"I'm trying," he snapped.

Fitting their chapped lips together again, he gave Natasha two more breaths. His right hand dropped and he fumbled with her sling. The contraption prevented him from getting to her sternum.

"Inhale," he demanded, worming his fingers beneath the strap.

Before he could push on her chest, she coughed.

Deep, jagged gasps wracked her body. She fell against him and he wrapped her with his free hand. Yanking his right one from between them, he pounded her back. She wasn't choking on anything, but he was helpless to do something.

Horrendous sobs interspersed with the gasps.

Lord Almighty, why? Did You forsake her too? The things this woman had lived through. She had been buried alive in a crushing pink tomb.

He shuddered, closing his mind before it attempted to feel what she described.

Her forehead ground into his chest, pushing her hat upward. Wretched heaving tortured her body, her lungs still not processing air.

"Slow down," he demanded, his vision blackening as his own breathing started matching hers. "You're hyperventilating. Slow down."

Ragged wails screamed into his coat as she cried and panted, fighting for breath and battling grief.

Ominous creaking rode on the wind, raising the hair on his arms.

"Woof, woof, woof." Lexi faced the direction Natasha had been traveling.

What now? He'd rather not find out.

Without asking permission, he gathered Natasha in his arms and picked her up. His ribs wailed and he saw spots but he was determined to protect her. He wished he had a free hand to adjust her hat, but he didn't. Sleet slapped her face, reddening her skin.

Natasha still gasped and struggled, but the jostling must have helped. She wasn't heaving as deeply.

"Slow breaths," he reminded her, not sure if she even heard him.

"Lexi," she cried, thrashing wildly in his arms.

"Stop." He lurched, trying not to drop her.

Her fists flailed and she bowed. *"Lexi."*

"Wooof, woof, woooof." The dog lifted her snout as far as she could.

"I killed her," Natasha croaked, her throat no longer supporting her voice. A tormented howl pierced his ears as she folded in on herself.

"Lexi's fine." He tripped on debris, loosening his tenuous hold. Muscling her back in place, he righted himself.

Thunder rolled across the dark sky, competing with the spruces bowing to the gale forces.

Twigs, branches, debris, and other potentially lethal objects sailed past them.

He needed to find shelter. Could he make it to the plane? Exhaustion and pain gave him less than a 50 percent chance. Did he dare enter the forest? Trees could be yanked from the ground, and a wealth of deadly detritus could impale them any second.

He had to decide. Now.

A grinding, rasping sound boomed across the opening. Turning, he shouted, stumbling backward in his haste to get away. A massive black shadow grew closer, falling from the sky.

Lexi barked and howled, turning every few feet as she fled.

Pivoting, he curled Natasha close, ignoring her screech of pain. *Run, run, run.*

His instincts screamed for him to run faster. *Go. Go. GO.*

WHOMP. The ground shook, and he stumbled. Managing to stay upright, he whirled to find the top of a massive spruce where he, Natasha, and Lexi had been seconds ago.

Plane, his mind barked, ending the quibbling for good.

Natasha jolted awake. Her eyes felt as raw as her throat. Blinking rapidly didn't do much to clear the crusty bleariness.

Every cell *ached* and her mind wanted to sink into the blackness again.

Wham. Something smacked…

Where was she? Forcing her eyes to clear, she frowned at the all-encompassing darkness. Night had finally conquered the long day. How long had she been asleep—passed out, more accurately?

Blinking did nothing to help her see. She cautiously slid her left hand off her hip and probed the surface beneath her. Softness like cloth. No, wait. Her fingertips stuttered over a rough line, then encountered smooth and cold like…leather?

It took her sluggish mind too long to realize she was inside the Cessna.

Wind howled and slammed into the plane.

A snort below her had her startling. Jerking up to her left elbow, she winced at the sudden movement. *Owww-wwwwwww.* Her ribs railed and her fractured collarbone stabbed its displeasure.

Gritting her teeth, she peered down. Nothing but more darkness. "Ian?"

Whoa. Was that her voice? She sounded like she had consumed sandpaper. The super coarse kind. Repeatedly.

She tried to swallow only to find her mouth so parched her tongue burned and stuck to her gums and roof. Water. She desperately needed water.

Another snort.

Since her fingers didn't smack into the instrument panel or yoke, she pictured Ian's large body curled on the floor in front of the row Lexi had traveled on. The storm probably took advantage of the broken windshield, soaking the front, but no moisture smacked her in this little oasis. Just sporadic puffs of wind iced damp clothes still clinging to her.

A soft whine mewled from Natasha's right.

"Lexi," she rasped, lying on her back.

Scrabbling nails and shuffling echoed, then a big, black-furred head shoved between the small V of the two seat backs, meeting Natasha's hand.

"Hey, girl." Natasha exhaled at the dizziness fuzzing her head.

She had no recollection of venturing back to the plane. The only clear memory was the flashback. She'd dropped into that nightmare, reliving it over again.

A single tear escaped and she dashed it away, angry she couldn't get past the tragedy. The first week in the hospital had been horrible. She had lived more in her head than reality. A psychologist tried to talk to her at her bedside, but she shut the man out. If she couldn't have Lexi beside her, she wanted to be alone. Nobody listened. Thankfully. Visitors steadily streamed into her room, and her parents had become fixtures, barely leaving.

Thanks to everyone pulling her out of the depression and grief, her PTSD episodes had become rare...until now.

To this day, she couldn't stand the sight of pink. It didn't matter the shade, the moment she saw it, she lost the ability to think coherently. And she hated the weakness.

Scratching her prickly scalp, she realized her hat was gone. A sense of loss panged her heart. It was irrational. She didn't know how she could mourn a baseball cap, but she did. She'd bought the hat on the last family vacation. The final one where her, her two older brothers, and her parents were together.

Her hand fisted. Another loss she laid at Randy Puckett's feet. Trivial compared to everything else, but a loss just the same.

"Nat?" a sleepy male voice rumbled. "You awake?"

Mortification scorched her cheeks, neck, and ears, spreading down her chest. How did she face him? He had witnessed a full-blown flashback. Not only that, she had also fallen apart, utterly broke down in his arms. Even in the hospital, she hadn't experienced such a shattering, such an utter rendering of weakness and desolation.

As a woman in a male-dominated field, showing anything less than strength and conviction spelled the end of garnering respect.

And she'd done just that with Ian. The pilot who had no problem showing just how much he resented accepting her charter. Had he been disgusted? Did he pity her now? Was he going to treat her like an invalid incapable of doing anything?

Why did she think sharing what happened would convince—

Her instincts detected movement out of the corner of her eye. Snapping her gaze that way was useless with the darkness, but a second later, Ian's fingers clutched her shoulder.

With the wind shaking the metal fuselage, she felt like she was on a demented carnival ride. If she survived this trip, she was *never* visiting an amusement park or fair again.

Ian cleared his throat. "It still smells like a juice farm had a party in here."

A bark of laughter tore out of her sore throat. His repeating her comment was so unexpected.

Chapter Twenty

Ian had no clue what to do. Did he ask if she was okay? Of course she wasn't. Who would be? But that was the polite response, wasn't it? Not saying anything could be conceived as callous, right? He was the worst at providing comfort. His ex-fiancée complained about his obtuseness and habit of trying to fix everything instead of listening.

Well. He had listened to Natasha's horrific story. Now what?

He shifted to relieve the ache in his shoulder. It didn't work. His physique wasn't made for this tiny space. He felt like a discarded pretzel, rotting on the floor. His clothes weren't sopping, but they weren't dry either. At the rate he was going, he'd start molding to add a fresh, fun layer of misery.

Something jabbed the top of his head and he swiped at it. A piece of plastic, most likely from the instrument panel, disappeared beneath the pilot seat. Grief shot through him, but nothing else. Natasha's nightmare cured him of any lingering remnants of anger and betrayal. If he were in her shoes, he probably would've done the same thing.

"I, uh, found this." He let go of her shoulder and slapped the metal floor, searching for...*gotcha.* "The Mafia missed it when they cleaned us out."

The twenty-ounce water bottle crinkled as he lifted it like an offering. "I, um, already had some." He couldn't help himself. When his shin discovered it the hard way, he fell on it like a lost man in a desert finding an oasis.

"What?"

He cringed at her husky, dry voice. It sounded so painful.

In the absolute darkness, it took him two tries to fit the bottle into her left hand. A soft cry rasped and he understood. He'd been beyond thirsty too.

"Hold it there," he instructed, letting go. "I'll twist the cap off." The moment he did, clothing rustled, then chugging.

The luminous hands on his watch were almost too faded to read. He squinted and found over six hours had passed since he sheltered them in the plane. Dawn was on the cusp, only an hour or so away. He doubted they'd see sunlight. The way the wind banged into the remnants of the Cessna, the back edge of the storm still blanketed the area. At least the rain and sleet had stopped.

"Thank you."

Natasha's soft words broke into his wandering thoughts. His pounding headache had lessoned but not disappeared. He blamed most of it on the concussion, but he was starving and still dehydrated. Those factors didn't help.

He bit his chapped lip. The water had absorbed into more important organs and areas than his lips. Nightmares still lingered, only *he* was the one trapped in the pink, hardening foam instead of Natasha. "Can I ask a question?"

He could *feel* her tense. "I don't mean to be insensitive," he forged ahead, "but I can't stop thinking about what you went through."

Stillness above him.

"How did the foam nozzles end up in the vestibule?" His scratchy voice bounced around the fuselage.

A long breath blew out of her. "I asked the same thing," she rasped.

Lexi whined, her nails clicking on the metal flooring. She hadn't been happy when he forced her behind Natasha's row, but he wanted to be ready if Natasha had another stop-breathing episode.

"The fire department cut me out." Plastic crinkled. "God had me covered. Departments from all over the city responded to the bombing." Her voice was barely above a whisper. "Witnesses called 9-1-1 so it took less than a minute for a crew to start sawing and axing me free."

He sat up, relishing the ability to stretch his legs by utilizing the space within the seat frame. The way his knees creaked and popped, someone would think he was older.

Clothing rustled with Natasha's movements. "When I woke up in the hospital, one of the guys—"

Ian assumed she meant one of the other officers at her station.

"—let it slip they were investigating the building."

He leaned forward. "As a lifelong construction worker, I can tell you for a fact that a foaming security system in a public vestibule is not normal."

Another snort. "No, it's not. Only criminals install the lethal option, which looks to be the case here. When I left Philadelphia, forensic accounting still hadn't uncovered the building's owners, but the layers they've peeled through point to Russians, possibly the same Mafia we're dealing with now."

He dropped his head. "Of course."

"I thought you were a pilot?"

Ian's chin snapped up at the change in topic. "I am."

"Not here," she rasped with a bite. "In Richmond."

His right hand clasped his left and squeezed. His big mouth just had to let that factoid slip in his need to keep a connection with her. And now he regretted it. Natasha trusted him enough to sob in his arms. She completely broke down and experienced PTSD to the point she almost suffocated herself.

He shuddered at the remaining dregs of terror and panic. She almost *died.* Again. In front of him. That hammered home just how invested he was in this woman.

Whoa. His heart blipped. He didn't just want to spend as much time as he could with her before she left…he didn't want her to leave him at all.

Wow. His gut had said she would change his life forever—

"Ace." She snapped her fingers, ripping him out of the mind-blowing epiphany.

"I worked construction full-time and flew in my off hours." The words were out before he had the thought, his mind still reeling from the revelation.

A grunt precipitated shifting. Natasha's boots banged on top of his legs. He jumped, not expecting the action, thanks to the total darkness.

"Sorry." The weight lifted, then clomped to the floor on either side of his thighs.

Heavy panting laced with pain followed and he understood. She had to be stiffer than him with all her injuries, and his muscles were like granite.

"You—"

"How can you still have faith in God after what you've been through?" He needed to throw her off probing into his background. No way did he want a dauntless officer who traveled to untamed Alaska on her own dime to capture a man based on shady information to learn that he'd been accused of smuggling. His ex-fiancée hadn't wanted his sullied reputation to affect her. Natasha, a law enforcement officer, would probably be even more conscious of the investigation.

For the first time in five months, he had a beautiful

woman treating him like a decent human being and possibly connecting with him. Something deep inside warmed, then cooled. He may have realized he liked Natasha far more than he wanted, but that didn't mean he had to confess anything. At least not yet. He would. Eventually. Maybe. If he had to. She had a full life in Philly and he had…a mess. How would they work?

Focus. Not that he wanted to discuss religion. Why did it have to be that topic slipping out?

Natasha squirmed. "You've mentioned faith more than once."

He wanted to fist pump the air. She'd taken the bait.

"I get you're not a fan—"

"It's hard to be when He sledgehammers lives and ignores prayers." Bitterness tinged the words.

"What happened?" she pressed.

The hole he dug was getting deeper. "Look at what happened to you for instance." He did his best to shift the focus.

Silence for three heartbeats.

His palms protested the nails burrowing in.

"You don't want to talk about your experience yet." Clothing rustled. "I won't press."

He bit his lip. The hurt in her tone stabbed his heart. Twice he opened his mouth, but fear robbed his voice. Natasha Greene mattered in ways his ex-fiancée never had. In the same way he had known that she would change his life forever, he just knew that he would never recover if she rejected him.

"God didn't abandon me that day. He did His best to protect me. He helped those firefighters cut me out in time. He helped the hospital staff keep me alive. And He still helps me, even when I don't realize it."

Ian rubbed the shame swirling in his chest. Of all the people he met, she should feel like him, but instead, her experience made her faith stronger. "But you're stranded in the middle of Alaska—"

"With you and Lexi," she cut in. "So far, the three of us have survived and conquered terrible things. That's not by chance."

Warmth stole through him. She included him on the same level as Lexi. He didn't deserve it, but he wouldn't argue. He wanted to feel good for a few more minutes. But he'd had enough religion for now. "Thank you for your candor and…" He scratched his beard. "I'll think about what you said."

"That's all I ask." Her heels hugged his thighs. "Do you know what time it is?"

He automatically twisted his wrist. "Um." The luminous hands on his watch were now barely legible. "Maybe four ten? I've run out of solar-power juice."

Wind bashed against the fuselage, rocking it like a metal band at a live concert.

His hand shot up to steady Natasha, only he punched her, swaying her forearm instead. "Sorry." He scrambled to grab on to her hand.

"Woof. Woof. Woof." Lexi's barking added a layer of tension.

A heavy body knocked against his right leg. He yanked his leg from underneath the seating to fold against his chest. Nails scrabbled against metal adding to the cacophony outside. Moments later, the German shepherd's head banged against his hip as she continued crawling beneath the seat frame.

"Lexi," he grumbled, pulling his right leg even harder against his chest to give her room to wiggle.

Another gust of wind buffeted the plane, throwing him aside as it lifted the wing still connected to the fuselage.

Natasha yelped, tightening her grip on his hand.

"Lexi, stay," Ian snapped, hoping the dog followed his order.

He yanked Natasha toward him.

She cried out, just as the plane's angle steepened.

For a single moment, they floated, suspended in midair as if someone pressed pause on a video.

Then that moment ended. Violently.

Another gale of wind blended with the first, shooting the wing upward.

"Hold on." He wrapped his arms around Natasha as best he could, given she wasn't fully off the seat.

The world flipped over at a dizzying rate.

Chapter Twenty-One

Randy jolted awake.

Grinding the bottom of his palms against his eye sockets, he silently groaned. It couldn't be time to wake up, but the alarm on his watch said otherwise.

Raging wind howled outside, worming its way through the cracks in the old hideout. It had been built ages ago to blend in with the surroundings. He doubted it had ever been updated or patched. It was a wonder it didn't collapse in the storm. Wet spots had sprung all over the place, thanks to the driving rain, adding a foul layer of rot.

Shivering, he cursed the primitive conditions.

The single-sized air mattress beneath him was no match for the king-size bed he had at home.

It's over. In a matter of hours, he'd leave this uncivilized section of the world and return to the compound deep in his beloved Pocono Mountains. The northeast region's militias had combined their resources and split the tasks to make the civil war happen. They had all finished their parts, and now he could finally start working on his: building the masterpieces to kick off the revolution. Once the Russians paid him.

His mood soured. He never wanted to work with the Mafia again. Pasha had become a complete despot. If

Randy had to listen to any more asinine orders in barely decipherable English, he was going to scream. The enforcer didn't handle stress well.

Instead of sending Andrei to search for the invaders, Pasha had set up a perimeter watch with scheduled rotations. Poor Vanya and Pyotr had been drafted into taking turns. Pasha tried to rope Randy into taking shifts, but Randy put his foot down. The deal between his militia and the Mafia was specific: the Russians provided security and the agreed-upon payment of explosives and supplies, Randy built bombs to their specifications.

He'd upheld his part. Time to go.

Dropping his hands, Randy used his abdomen muscles to sit up. A single battery-powered lamp sat on the scarred, round wooden table close to the kitchenette. Yawning, he forced his legs to stand up. He'd only fallen asleep a few hours ago. He'd pushed himself to finish the last set of bombs after thoroughly searching the confiscated items.

The worn packs yielded nothing beyond clothing and toiletries. No identification, cash, or credit cards within. The hunting rifle had been an interesting item but not surprising given the pilot landed in untamed areas. What had startled him was the satellite phone wedged between the first aid kit and emergency-rations bag when he initially combed through the pile.

His boots clomped across the unvarnished wooden slats. Stopping beside the table, he fingered the second-rate, ugly, orange-and-black device, probably bought off a wholesale internet site. The thick antennae was at least four inches tall and he bet it wasn't encrypted like his equipment. Either way, he grinned at the sight. Bet the pilot missed this *a lot*. It gave Randy hope that the two interlopers hadn't called for rescue or informed the police of his presence.

The grin fell away as his gaze shifted to the documents

spread on the surface. In one of the compartments in the plane, a gold mine of information had been stashed, including the registration information for the Cessna 180. It belonged to Ian Dalton with a Richmond, Virginia, address. How informative. *And* a confirmation of Randy's suspicion. Randy had hired Dalton, and the pilot had returned with a new passenger.

His gaze slid to two red, rubbery rectangles. The matching luggage had given him all he needed, thanks to the tags hanging from the handles. According to the handwriting on the lined cards within, Natasha Greene had flown to Alaska from Philadelphia. She even included a handy phone number.

The final item on the table had his hands fisting. A dog harness with K-9 officer markings.

Even if he hadn't heard Natasha's name endlessly spouted in the news, he'd have known exactly who she was. She was the officer who'd tried to catch him after he detonated the bomb near the Liberty Bell. She and her meddlesome K-9 had latched on to the courier en route to plant the device. Knowing the patsy would never make it, Randy initiated the blast so as not to lose the message completely: the Liberty Bell didn't represent freedom anymore. The government that supposedly freed them now oppressed them.

But that would change.

He skimmed the addresses of the two people who'd flown here to destroy everything. Ideas began percolating as he marched to the ancient coffeepot. The decrepit thing couldn't do more than warm water, so he was stuck with instant coffee. *Blech*. But caffeine was caffeine, no matter how nasty.

Stirring the tepid brew, he glanced at his watch. 4:21 a.m. Pennsylvania was four hours ahead. Not too early there to call his father. He wanted to let the militia leader know Randy had finished the contract with the Russians and to expect him home today. He also was curious to see what his father had dug up on Ian and Natasha. The officer was going to be harder to ruin, but not impossible. He already had a few possibilities in mind. Ian, on the other hand, had skeletons in his closet. Randy was sure of it. The vibe he'd gotten off pilot was desperation mixed with anger. He was hiding something, and Randy would know it soon. Then he'd decide how to proceed with wrecking their lives.

Pasha wandered into the kitchenette, yawning. "We change landing location."

Randy stopped stirring. "Why?"

"Wind." Pasha grabbed another chipped mug and filled it with warm water. "I have new coordinates. We leave soon to meet plane in time."

Relief had him offering a smile to the turncoat dictator. "I'll finish packing now."

The raging wind whooshed the Cessna's surviving wing upward.

Natasha screamed, the sound ripping out of her sore throat of its own volition. Slamming against Ian, she clung to the man like a barnacle.

The plane tilted almost straight up, tossing them against the ravaged frame.

Oomph. Air flew out of her lungs, and the side of her head thunked against something unforgiving.

Lexi squealed, but Natasha was helpless to do anything.

Her vision blurred and her surroundings swirled like a kaleidoscope.

Thwump. The Cessna flipped, tossing them with it.

Her senses overloaded.

A horrific crack drowned everything else, then the tail

of the plane sheared away. Raging air whirled inside, tugging at her clothes and tangling her hair around her face.

A section of the instrument panel soared past her cheek by centimeters. It crashed against the fuselage, then disappeared out of the new hole from the missing tail.

Ian hit the same spot as the instrument panel a moment later, but he managed to remain inside. She winced as her right shoulder and arm squished between them.

The wind whipped the Cessna sideways again, then hung.

One heartbeat. Two heartbeats. Three—

The plane smacked back down on its belly, the frame shuddering violently.

Ian's body-wracking groan shook Natasha and she added her own to the mix. Her brain wouldn't stop sloshing inside her skull.

Natasha didn't want to think about how they managed to land a foot from the jagged opening where the cargo hold and tail had been. One more flip, and they probably would've been tossed out of the plane. As it was, she had to climb off Ian. Now. The wind could toss the Cessna again at any moment.

Slapping a hand on the floor, she did her best to lift herself. Cells, bones, and organs wailed. She probably had bruises on everything, but she had to force herself not to faint. The black dots and white lights crowding her vision made it impossible to see clearly.

Big hands clamped on her hips, helping her rise.

"We…" Ian panted, "gotta…move."

"I know." She gave up trying to stand. Staying on her hand and knees, she swayed, blinking *a lot*, forcing three blurry holes into one image. "Lexi."

The dog whimpered just as her tail thumped against Natasha's forearm. Lexi had had the best seat on the deranged ride. She managed to stay beneath the seating frame, saving her from flying around like a popcorn kernel in a microwave bag.

Natasha crawled forward. She couldn't maintain a straight line and she didn't care. As long as she made it outside before the wind struck again, she considered it a win.

Chapter Twenty-Two

Ian bent, bracing both hands on his thighs. The battle with nausea raged strong, and he didn't know who would win. It was sixty-forty odds he'd lose.

Whatever healing he'd reaped from sleep had been destroyed. Piercing pain stabbed his brain, his skull felt like it'd lost a few rounds with a prize fighter, and his organs were scrambled like puzzle pieces in a box. He wasn't sure if they'd ever fit back in place.

"I never," Natasha rasped, "want to do…that again."

Agreed. He couldn't say it out loud or he'd forfeit the battle with his stomach. Tossing his cookies twice on this venture was two times too many, and he refused to add a third.

Lexi hobbled into his limited view. He made a mental note to ask Natasha about the one leg. He couldn't be sure with his brain still seesawing, but the dog looked out of balance.

Two giant gusts of wind swatted him, knocking him to the side.

Darkness still reigned over the landscape. No soft light from the moon or stars permeated the heavy clouds. Inside the plane, it had been suffocating, but in the open terrain, it was nerve-wracking. Everything appeared menacing and threw off his perception. Thankfully, dawn should begin any minute.

"Distract me," he managed to push between clenched teeth. He futilely pantomimed the contents from his stomach rising up and out to explain the demand. She probably couldn't see his effort.

"How?" Natasha shifted to just inside his peripheral vision.

"Family." Rolling his wrist, he hoped she got the message that he didn't care how she interpreted the topic. *Just talk.*

"Oh, um." Her husky voice hadn't had a chance to heal from her flashback, and he winced, hurting for her.

"Let's see." Her boots scraped against blueberry bushes.

The Cessna had landed most of the way up the steep hill closest to the Russians. It took a lot of effort and will-power to climb the rest of the way. Hence, his current predicament.

"I have two older brothers," she announced.

That explained so much. He was an only child, but he could just imagine what he'd be like to a little sister. Merciless during adolescence, then overbearing during high school years.

He motioned for more.

"Um." She cleared her throat. "Scott, the oldest, is also a police officer in Philadelphia. He's a sergeant in a different district, but that doesn't stop him from ordering me around."

So much aggravated affection laced those words.

"John's the middle child," she continued. "He's a fire-fighter stationed near the art museum. Sometimes, I run into him at scenes but, thankfully, not often."

Ian was glad to hear it. Since Lexi detected explosives, he didn't want to imagine the disaster the added layer of fire could cause.

"You probably think Mom and Dad are first responders too."

It crossed his mind.

"But they're not. Mom's a high school teacher and Dad is in management with a mortgage company."

Not what he expected.

"My brothers and I grew up on stories from my mom's father and her siblings." She launched into a grand story about her grandfather apprehending a ring of criminals.

He let the cadence of her words flow over him, and little by little, the nausea faded. His stomach stopped lurching and he finally could stand upright.

"Thank you," he stated when she finished. Wiping his sweaty face, he grimaced at the grime on his palms.

"What about you?"

Her question captured his full attention. "No siblings." He glanced at their surroundings. Dark lumps represented trees and shrubs.

"It was your uncle who taught you to fly?"

"Yes." He thumbed toward the shattered plane. "That was his Cessna. I bought it five months ago."

"Right before you moved here."

Warning, warning. Change the topic. "I'm not as versed in hunting criminals as you, but should we wait for daylight? I can't imagine finding the hideout in this." He motioned to the dark sky.

Natasha bit back the retort hovering on the edge of her lips. Once again, he cut off her questioning. What was he hiding?

She wanted to know, but she needed to find Randy. "Actually." She shuffled to face the correct direction. "We're going to take advantage of the darkness."

He jolted, his chin snapping her way. "How? We can barely see anything."

True. She'd never experienced darkness like this before. She always had lights from the city, and the few times she'd ventured to scenic places, light pollution from a nearby town offered illumination against the sky. But here, with no civilization anywhere close, *nothing* leached into the darkness.

She bet the stars were amazing. If only the clouds weren't in the way. But they were and she wasn't on vacation.

"Haven't you watched movies and TV?" she asked, mostly in jest. "All the best spies skulk in the dark."

"You very clearly told me you weren't a spy."

She lifted her chin, steeling her mind and body for the journey ahead. "You're right. I'm better."

"Wow." He held up his hands in surrender. "Your humility overwhelms me. Stop. I can't take it."

"I didn't travel all this way and endure so much just to lose him now." She planted a boot into the mud, ignoring the squish.

Ian fell in step beside her with Lexi between them.

"I've got something those second-rate spies wished they had." The boasting kept her mind off the agony running rampant inside.

"Yeah?" His boots splashed muck and leaves. "What's that?"

"Lexi."

The dog snapped her attention to Natasha, waiting for a command or reason for the use of her name.

"Who better to find a bomb maker's lair than a dog—"

"Who detects explosives," Ian finished, respect layering his tone. "Impressive, Officer Greene. Very impressive."

Her cheeks warmed and she couldn't stop the sloppy grin filling her face. Dazzling Ian Dalton should not be on her to-do list, but she couldn't help it. She liked the way he gave her props. His praise also went a long way in soothing her fears about her PTSD attack. So far, he hadn't treated her any differently than before or looked at her with pity.

You're allowing him to distract you again.

"Go to work," she commanded Lexi, using the phrase along with a hand signal to start the hunt for explosives.

The dog immediately shifted into work mode and began limp-trotting.

Natasha couldn't keep up with the German shepherd, but as long as she kept tabs on the dog's tail, she was okay following at a steady—fine, slow—pace. Ian started out beside her, but the thickening forest forced him to walk behind her. By the visible bruises and the way he periodically held his ribs, she didn't think he minded pulling up the rear.

With every passing minute, the surrounding darkness became less dense. With the storm's clouds still blanketing the sky, dawn couldn't show off its dazzling array of colors and she felt cheated. Just like the stars at night, she bet the sunrise in this untamed place was amazing.

Natasha paused to reach into her sling— "Oh no," she whispered.

"What?" Ian responded in a low voice.

"I lost my cell phone." First her hat, now her phone had been sacrificed on this trip to unearth Randy Puckett. Inane, small things, but the attachment value was high.

"I, uh, guess it's a good time to mention," he added, still whispering, "I don't have either of the rifles."

Her gaze shifted to his shoulders. How had she missed that? Normally, her fanatical attention to detail would've caught that right away.

"I took them off when I tucked into the tiny space on the floor."

"And the tumbling plane ride tossed them who knows where," she finished, then blew out a breath.

"Yep."

Heading to her enemy's hideout unarmed was insane. "Wait." She faced Ian. "Don't you have a revolver?" A Smith & Wesson .44 Magnum if she recalled right.

He gaped. "I didn't think you saw that. You hadn't mentioned it."

What was the big deal? Was it illegal? Did he not have a permit? At the moment, she didn't care. As long as it worked, she'd embrace ignorance. "How many bullets do you have?"

"Six loaded in the cylinder, but no extras. My ammunition boxes were taken when the Mafia confiscated our stuff."

Figured. She restarted the journey through the muck. "We'll have to make it work. I'm not planning on confronting them."

"What are you planning?"

"Sneak in and find my satellite phone." She plodded on. "Learn their plans, if possible, then get out."

He snorted. "Sure. No problem."

She'd take the sarcasm. He didn't balk, outright refuse to help, or run the other way. Win.

Chapter Twenty-Three

Natasha hated nature. She hadn't known that about herself, but this trip had taught her nature had a mean streak.

Wind thrashed the vegetation with no rhyme or reason. She couldn't anticipate—or dodge—flying debris or know when bushes, branches, and shrubs twisted to slap her.

"Ow." Her hand flew to the top of her head. Another branch from some unknown shrub tangled in her loose hair for the third time. Grabbing the offending vegetation, she pulled her strands free of the diabolical leaves. At this rate, she'd be bald by the time they found the hideout.

"Here."

An object plopped on top of her head. Her fingers raised, smacking the brim of a hat. She pivoted to find Ian finger combing his in-need-of-a-cut locks.

"Hold up." He plucked his hat back off, fiddled with the sizing, then dropped it onto her head again. "Better."

It was. He'd guessed the size just right. That connection deep inside her sighed at the thoughtful gesture. She had to wrangle her mind into taking over, stopping herself from filling with sappy musings of romance in their future.

Clearing her throat, she gestured. "Can you?" Her cheeks flamed for needing the aid, but she didn't want to stop too long. She'd already lost full darkness. If the sun rose too much more, she might as well give up any hope of stealth. "Help. My hair."

"Oh, right."

It took the two of them a few tries to work together, but they finally fed her hair through the hole in the back and the hat settled firmly in place.

"Thank you." She whirled so he didn't catch the embarrassing grin taking over her face.

Resuming her pace, Ian, once again, filled her thoughts instead of the mission ahead. She was getting glimpses of a caring, thoughtful man beneath the surface-level charisma. She didn't like that she noticed. She had to remain focused. Catching Randy Puckett came first. And yet, the connection that had sparked when they first met had its own agenda.

When she woke up in the plane, she thought for sure he'd treat her differently. He'd witnessed a PTSD episode. How could he not see her as less? Yet, he hadn't.

Not true. He had changed, only not how she expected. He'd lost the angry chip on his shoulder and the constant frown.

All her life, she had fought to be taken seriously. To be seen as an equal, not a woman in a "man's" role. Her brothers did it, her grandfather and uncles did it, the guys at the station did it. Maybe they didn't realize it, but she worked twice as hard to gain respect and knew she could lose it any second.

But none of that happened with Ian. Not once had he treated her like a brainless female or an annoying invalid, even with her obvious handicap. He'd never assumed she couldn't do something based on her injuries or owning a pair of ovaries. His concern was always safety-based— avoiding the storm, escaping the Mafia, surviving a possible showdown—but never about her endurance or lack thereof.

Wow. The realization hit her hard. No wonder her thoughts kept circling back to the man. Her palms grew clammy. She hadn't come to Alaska for anyone other than Randy, but God had thrown Ian in her path and she had to listen.

No, she did not. Ripping a boot out of clingy long grass, she rechanneled her focus. As she stated before, she hadn't come all this way and endured so much to come up empty-handed. If she didn't keep her head in the mission, she'd lose her opportunity to capture the bomb maker.

Her jaw tightened.

A twig snapped beneath her foot and she cringed. With the howling wind, the clacking branches, and rustling leaves, the snapped twig shouldn't be heard by anyone, but still. A professional didn't make rookie mistakes. Not that she had much—zero—wilderness training.

Lexi lifted her head, stopping.

Natasha held her hand up to halt Ian. He paused right behind her.

Lexi peered at Natasha.

Natasha gave hand signals for Lexi to move silently and show what she'd found.

The dog slunk forward, swerving toward the right. As she approached a space equidistant between two trees, her pace became glacial.

Puffs of air hit Natasha's neck just as Ian whispered, "What'd she find?"

Natasha lifted her left shoulder, telling him she didn't know. But her stomach tightened with suspicion.

Lexi's belly hit the soggy ground, facing forward. She cranked her head to peer back at Natasha.

Natasha silently praised her partner and motioned for the dog to stay in place. "Ian," she whispered over her shoulder. "Don't move."

He stiffened.

"I mean it," she reiterated. "I have to find out what she discovered, but I need you to remain behind."

"Why?" he demanded softly.

He probably figured Lexi lying down was a signal. She didn't blame him for wanting to understand as much as possible. She'd want to know if the roles were reversed.

"There could be a bomb," she responded bluntly to press home the seriousness. "I don't want you setting it off."

His muscles turned to granite and he swayed. She bet the color drained from his face too, but she didn't bother checking. Lexi had her full attention.

Taking his statuesque stance as confirmation he'd stay put, Natasha crept forward as carefully as she could. Having Lexi as her partner for four years taught Natasha a lot. One of the most valuable lessons was to walk exactly where the dog had. That pathway was cleared by an expert and Natasha was smart enough to know not to veer from it.

By the time Natasha reached her partner's side, sweat rimmed her borrowed hat. Impressive, given the cold temperature and driving winds. Maneuvering to sit on the frigid ground took a lot of graceless jostling and hip jiving. Ian better not say a word.

At first, she didn't see anything. The ambient light didn't illuminate like the sun, but it was strong enough not to need a flashlight. Which she didn't have. Or use the flashlight app on her phone. Which she'd lost. But, whatever. They'd give away her position to anyone watching anyway.

There, a disturbance in the ground was unlike its surroundings. Someone had dug a hole, then refilled it.

The spruces' bottom branches swayed dangerously close, sometimes almost slapping the potential hazard. The pounding rain and the vibrations of the branches meant the sensitivity on the bomb—and she was positive Randy had buried that fun treasure for her to detonate the wrong way—was low. It probably needed direct weight to explode.

Solace to all the unsuspecting animals in the area.

Was that all? She crouched lower, ignoring her screaming injuries. Squinting, she searched from the ground upward, centimeter by centimeter. *Bingo.* Straightening, she gasped at the raging pain lancing through her. Blinking against the black dots in her vision, she fought the rush of dizziness.

"Nat?"

She grimaced at Ian's hoarse whisper. She had never dealt with the Russian Mafia before, so she didn't know how vigilant they were. Did they establish security perimeters with manned personnel? Were there enough men for that? She'd seen four after the plane first crashed. How many had stayed behind?

Using the tree to stand, she made her way back to Ian. Crowding into his space, she yanked on his coat until he bent low enough that she could talk into his ear. "Lexi found a bomb."

He startled, snapping his gaze toward her partner.

"I found a trip wire about seven inches off the ground."

A large hand wrapped around her left bicep and squeezed.

"I'm sure the bomb has a pressure plate," she continued, needing him to understand the severity of the situation. "It either detonates once you step on it, or the moment you step off. I'm betting on the latter, given the uncontrolled environment."

"Seriously?" he whispered.

"Yep." Natasha sent up a prayer for help. "From here on out, no talking."

He pulled back and searched her face.

What he found, she had no clue, nor did she care. Their safety depended on her judgments. She couldn't fail.

"You think they've set up a watch, like they did with my Cessna?"

Astute. Ian kept proving he was observant and smart.

"I can't say for sure, but it's a possibility." One that made her stomach gurgle. "I don't want to tip anyone off, just in case."

"Neither do I."

"I'll be following Lexi." She tugged his coat to make sure he paid attention. "Step *only* where we step, got it?"

He swallowed. Hard. "Got it," he rasped.

She disentangled herself and turned. "Time to find a path through the minefield."

Chapter Twenty-Four

Ian had trouble focusing. His breathing kept veering toward hyperventilating and he consciously had to stop himself. If passing out didn't give them away to a potential guard, his heavy panting would. Natasha was going to send him back to the ravine if he didn't calm down.

A part of him hoped that happened, but the rest of him balked at the thought of her searching the wilderness by herself. A shudder rippled down his spine. The recollection of the wolves setting up for an attack liquefied his guts. He always thought of himself as a tough guy, but this wretched journey had shown him otherwise. But seriously. Who, outside trained police and military, dealt with bombs planted in the woods? Or assault-rifle-wielding Mafia?

Carefully placing his boot where Natasha had stepped a moment ago, he wondered how his life had gone so wrong. *No. No wondering anything.* He had to stay vigilant.

Lexi had scented three more bombs, all buried in prime places between pairs of trees.

How did Natasha deal with the stress? Sweat soaked his hair, and his body wouldn't stop trembling.

He needed to eat. Hunger didn't help his anxiety, but he couldn't do anything about that now.

Lexi lay on her stomach again.

Oh man. He halted, scrubbing his face. His beard scratched his palms and he didn't care about the grime. His only purpose was to not distract Natasha and be on the lookout for the Mafia itching to press their triggers.

Natasha repeated the same process as before. She crept to the dog, sat on the ground, then inspected the area intensely.

Snapping his head up, Ian cocked an ear. Had he heard something?

The wind refused to quit. It kept blustering, shaking and rattling everything, including his nerves.

Turning in a slow circle, he squinted into the gray light. Nothing looked different from before. The spruces danced and rustled. The weeds and shrubs shook and bent.

He kept circling in place—

There. He heard it again. A muffled thump. Straining, he tried to tune out the environment. The thump was rhythmic. Footsteps.

"Psssst." He signaled as softly, yet with enough punch, as he could.

Natasha cranked her head toward him, expression full of fury.

She'd be more upset if the guard got the drop on them. He pantomimed someone was coming.

Her expression morphed into alarm and she searched, but her position was too low for her to see much.

Against the protocol of hanging back after Lexi alerted, he marched forward, ensuring he stepped in the path he'd memorized.

"What are you doing?" she hissed when he crouched behind her.

"Carrying you." He shoved a hand under her knees and smoothed the other against her back. "We don't have time for you to stand."

"Be careful," she snapped into his ear, making his eardrum ring. "Trip wire a foot in front of me."

His brain fizzed for a second. "Show me where to go."

Rising, he gritted his teeth against the slicing in his ribs and head. She wasn't heavy, but his injuries made it difficult, and he didn't have as much adrenaline running through him this time.

"Lexi." She made a complicated signal.

The dog's ears swiveled, then locked on to the sound. She rose and began trotting a different bearing.

"Follow Lexi," Natasha breathed.

He had no problem with adrenaline now. If he placed his foot in the wrong spot, he'd kill them instantly. Panic rose, leeching out in a cold sweat. He couldn't let hysteria win.

Heavy footsteps thumped louder.

"He's catching up." Natasha searched behind Ian.

His pulse ratcheted. He needed to hide. Where? Where did he go? What was safe? His steps faltered and he stumbled. *No.* He clutched Natasha tighter. Bomb. He couldn't drop her on a bomb.

His vision tunneled and he squeezed. Finally finding his balance, his gaze roved. Where was Lexi? He lost the dog. How did he know where to step?

"Drop," Natasha ordered against his lobe.

He didn't think, he just crouched beside an overgrown thicket of Bebb's willows.

"Don't move." Her words were so low, he could barely hear them over his thundering pulse.

His nerves coiled tighter. How much more could they twine before they broke?

A dead branch thunked from a boot hitting it.

He stilled. Or tried to. His trembling body refused to still.

"Loosen…your…grip," Natasha rasped against him.

He instantly complied, horrified he had been squeezing so hard. He had to get it together. She needed a partner, not a man on the verge of a nervous breakdown.

Bushes shook on the other side of the Bebb's willow,

moved by more than the gusts of the wind. He couldn't see anything, but his instincts told him the threat was close.

Fresh cigarette smoke shot up his nose and he scrunched it in disgust. Uncaring if Natasha thought him a creeper, he tucked his nose against her throat and inhaled. She smelled so much better and didn't make him want to gag or sneeze.

She did the same to him. He just hoped he didn't make her choke.

Frustration fed into his edginess. He wanted to see who stood so near. Was it one of the two men they'd already tangled with? He hoped so but doubted it. Those two were injured. A guard needed to be healthy, right?

Another waft of cigarette smoke drifted over them.

Ian had already proven he'd protect Natasha and Lexi, he just didn't want to become an animal again. The uncontrollable rage directing his actions scared him. He had no concept of right or wrong, only survival at *all* costs.

Natasha shifted and wiggled in his arms. He lost his grip and almost dropped her. Scrambling to reestablish the hold, she ignored him and wormed her fingers through the Bebb's willow's thicket of branches, but she didn't get far. The mass was too tangled to make a hole.

Something sizzled as another stream of smoke blew above them, drifting down.

Heavy boot steps began a steady thump, their pace unhurried. Better yet, moving away from their spot.

Ian exhaled, the immense relief making him giddy.

"Put me down," she whispered.

Ian's anxious mind followed her demand exactly. He bent and let go.

She splatted in muck.

"Oh." He hadn't dropped her, but he couldn't believe he'd just set her in a thick puddle. "I'm sorry."

"Sure you are," she muttered, whacking his coat. "Do you think you can help me stand without an issue?"

Keeping his mouth closed at the deserved jab, he supported her ungainly rise upward.

Lexi trotted around a different set of bushes, her tongue hanging out of the side of her large mouth. Right after the three of them had escaped the flipping plane, the dog arrowed for the stream and lapped quite a bit before Natasha stopped her.

He hoped Lexi had swallowed enough to quench her thirst. He wished he had joined her.

"Now we know there's at least one guard on duty." Natasha swiped at the dripping mud coating the back of her with no success. "Let's take advantage of our window."

Window? He didn't ask. She knew what she was doing. That was good enough.

Heading in the opposite direction of the receding footsteps, they fell in tandem behind the German shepherd. It didn't take long before Lexi dropped to her belly.

Natasha beckoned for the dog to sniff a different area nearby. Lexi did as commanded but didn't lie down. Nat smiled. With visible effort, she began to lower.

He charged forward. "Stop," he whispered, as he clasped her forearm.

She froze, her gaze flying to his. Alarm blazed from her eyes as she silently mouthed "what's wrong?"

"Tell *me* what to look for." He forced her to stand. "I can sit on the ground easier." Lie, but he couldn't handle seeing her in so much pain.

She bit her lip, then nodded. "Look for a straight line about six-to-nine inches from the ground. It's black, so it'll be hard to spot, but you should see it if you concentrate. I'm trying to find out if there's a continuous trip wire or if it's been placed in sections."

His stomach quivered. He suddenly didn't want the responsibility. If he missed the wire, he'd kill them all.

No defeatist thinking allowed, his mind reprimanded. Dropping to his hands and knees, he lowered his head.

Nope. No good. Maneuvering sideways, he twisted his neck and used his elbows to rest his weight. Better.

Lexi pressed against him, her pants puffing in his ear.

"Don't distract me," he muttered, staring hard at the space in front of him. He didn't see anything. Lifting a hand and knee, he carefully sidled closer sideways. Still nothing.

"I don't see anything." He was too terrified to look away from his task.

"I don't either."

Ian jolted and just barely bit back a squeak. Snapping his face forward, he found Natasha crouched, fighting for space with a sitka spruce.

How did he not hear her or that racket?

"Woman," he whisper-barked. "I want back those ten years you just took."

His heart lodged in his throat. He couldn't take much more of this. The Russians didn't have to bother shooting him, his heart was going to give out.

She grinned, the smile lighting up her face.

Beautiful. "Brat." He ruefully grinned as he sat on his heels and combed shaking hands through his hair.

"Come on, Ace." She used him to stand. "We found an opening. Step one is complete."

He wanted to grumble about the nickname, but he secretly liked how she teased him with it, liked the exclusive connection.

Hoisting himself upward, his rubbery legs threatened to buckle. "I'm afraid to ask about step two."

"Find the hideout." Her expression grew determined. "Step three—sneak in."

Chapter Twenty-Five

Natasha wanted to tear her hair out and bellow at the sky.

Dawn had come and gone with daylight now fully in charge. The clouds might not allow sunshine, but the gray day had plenty of light chasing the shadows. Too much light. She was back to depending on the variety of flora to hide their presence.

So far, she hadn't spotted any cameras, but that didn't mean anything. The forest was so dense with potential anchor points, she probably missed them all if they existed.

They hadn't run into another guard, but it was only a matter of time before that changed.

They had to pick up the pace. The longer she wove through the trees, the more time Randy had to escape. Or notice them.

Lexi lay on her stomach.

Natasha gnashed her teeth. She'd lost count of the number of bombs planted in the ground. How did the Mafia roam the area? A safe passage to the hideout obviously existed, she just hadn't found the key to uncovering it. Yet.

She sure found everything else.

Lexi not only searched for the bombs, she revealed the trip wires too. It took a little time for Natasha to train the dog, but Lexi's intelligence was amazing, and it was worth it. The German shepherd was the perfect height and had much better eyesight to find the thin, deadly lines.

The clock ticking inside Natasha's head ticked louder.

Motioning for Lexi to keep searching, the dog rose and wound a different path between the trees.

Natasha peered over her shoulder to check on Ian. He nodded grimly, his eyes latching on to hers from the spot Lexi had just left. The man had become adept at staying on Natasha's heels without crowding. He hadn't said a word since she laid out her simplistic plan and she was grateful.

Her nerves were wound so tight, she might scream if they didn't find Randy soon.

Lexi stopped but didn't signal. Her snout remained forward as she sniffed the air.

Hope blossomed in Natasha's chest. *This is it.* She could feel it. Creeping to the dog's side, she scratched between Lexi's ears.

Lexi sniffed Natasha's coat pocket, searching for her reward. Remorse dashed the hope. Natasha didn't have the cross-eyed crocodile. She'd packed it in the luggage, believing she'd have time to equip for the search. Lexi deserved the toy plus a whole box of treats for the number of bombs and wires she'd detected.

Soon, she mouthed to the dog, willing her partner to understand. Once she snuck inside, she'd reclaim the toy and satellite phone. Everybody won.

Shifting her attention forward, Natasha scoured the area for the hideout. Nothing but trees and dense vegetation, then it hit her. Disguised. The structure had to be hidden within the mass.

Hope resurged along with nerves. She was so close. Randy wouldn't get away this time.

Ian crowded against her back, blocking the wind buffeting her wet pants. "This it?" he whispered against her ear, his beard scratching her lobe.

She shivered and nodded.

Lexi stopped waiting for her toy and put her nose on the ground. She wandered forward, then turned right when she reached a density of flora.

Natasha followed, brushing her left hand against a patch of stalks bound tightly together. Wait. She stopped. Worming her fingers between a set of green and brown branches, she beamed at what she found beneath. Slats of wood.

Yes. Adrenaline soared in her veins, making her feel invincible. *YES.* No more guessing. She had found the hideout.

Ian peered over Natasha's shoulder and gaped. Wood, crudely cut into long boards, peeked between the shrubs cleverly placed to hide the wall.

Natasha had done it. She'd found the lair.

Fear grabbed him by the throat. On the other side of this barrier, at least two angry Russians wanted to exact revenge on Ian and Lexi.

With bullets. A barrage of them.

He had trouble swallowing.

Traipsing through a bomb-riddled forest had been hard enough without creeping up on a building full of men out to kill them.

His boot broke through a thicket of alder scrub growing rampant everywhere. Overgrown bushes and ferns had multiplied out of control. They claimed every centimeter of available ground for their own. They'd already overtaken the hideout's wall, and soon they'd strangle the spruces towering nearby.

Ian hoped Randy hadn't planted a bomb this close to the refuge, but he couldn't count on it. A guy heartless enough to set off a bomb at the Liberty Bell and take advantage of a deadly security system to trap Natasha and Lexi could easily rig the place to blow as a fail-safe.

Ian's gut tightened and he fisted his hands to prevent them from holding Natasha back. Lexi hadn't alerted, so he had to keep moving. Or try to. He ripped his boot out of the alder and swiped at the leaves tangling in his hair.

A few feet ahead, Natasha ducked back, her left shoulder hitting a thick stalk.

Ian's heart shot into his throat and he instantly froze. Searching for a reason, he scanned ahead. Dancing branches and flying debris, thanks to the wind, circled and clacked. No visible threat.

He inched closer, wincing at the creaks and snaps beneath his tread. Cold sweat coated his underarms and hands, freezing his body every time a gust took advantage of a gap in his jacket.

Natasha carefully twisted to flatten her front against the wall. He reached her just as she began to bend at the waist toward her right.

What is she doing? He stopped behind her, his coat brushing her back.

She startled and fell against him.

He shunted power into his stance to brace her unexpected weight. Keeping them upright, his hands dropped to her hips to help her balance. She didn't seem to notice his efforts. She began leaning again, so he did too.

Whoa. A window with real glass. Someone had built a frame from the same wood as the wall to fit the two-by-two-and-a-half-foot glass that remained stationary. It didn't open, but that probably didn't matter to the occupants inside.

Natasha's breath caught.

Ian ripped his attention away from the coarse construction to peer at the view beyond the pane. He sucked in air.

The primitive room had slat-wood floors and ceiling. A tiny kitchenette spread across the back corner with a round wooden table close by. He recognized most of the contents covering the surface.

Dread and fury welled. His Cessna's documentation had all his information including his Richmond address. The bomb maker knew where he lived.

"My satellite phone," Natasha whispered under her breath.

His gaze jumped to the large orange-and-black device resting beside two red luggage tags—

An engine roared to life.

"No." Natasha pushed him back.

He lost his balance and tripped, clearing just enough space for her to turn.

The cast on her upper right arm clocked him in the temple as she flailed to free herself from the alder scrub.

Two more engines growled into existence. Then a fourth.

"Move," she yelled, fighting the vegetation.

He didn't know whether she shouted at him or the plants, but he did his best to get out of the way. His skull rang and throbbed as he attempted to stay upright.

Lexi ran out of a copse of bushes behind him and limp-hustled along the side of the wall.

Natasha freed her legs, stomping them into the soggy bog that had formed in the storm. With a speed he hadn't known she was capable of, she rushed after Lexi.

The dog disappeared around a corner. Seconds later, so did Natasha.

He kicked at the ferns and alder, stumbling after the pair like a toddler learning to walk.

Finally reaching the corner, he flung his hand out to grasp the edge and whipped around to find chaos.

Chapter Twenty-Six

"Randy Puckett," Natasha bellowed, running as fast as she could.

Brake lights on the last four-wheel, all-terrain vehicle—ATV—blinked, then remained red as it rolled to a stop between a set of trees.

The man sitting astride the long black seat let go of the handlebar and twisted. His smug face grinned, then he gave her an insolent salute.

"No," she bellowed, trying to erase the distance between them. Pure determination fueled her to succeed and ignore her body's warnings to stop.

Lexi howled and increased her pace, gaining ground.

The smile dropped away and Randy turned forward. With a twist of his wrist, he gave the ATV gas and disappeared between the trees. The single headlight cut through the gloom, providing Natasha the only visible marker until it, too, disappeared.

"No. No. NO." Her throat tore at the shouts. He couldn't get away. Not again. She pushed herself to continue running.

Lexi broke off the chase with a yelp. She limp-pivoted and walked back to Natasha, her back leg lifted off the ground.

The sight broke Natasha's heart and released the rage caged inside.

"He *cannot* win." She whirled. "He *will not* win."

Ian halted his run, gaping at her.

"Move, Ace." She swished her slinged hand, indicating he needed to comply *now.*

He didn't even twitch. The obtuse man stood between her and the flapping back door.

"I will run you over." Her pace didn't slow. She wasn't stopping until she got inside.

Lexi caught up and started barking.

"Even my partner wants you out of the way." Natasha gauged the twenty feet between her and Ian. She had enough room to go around if she had to, but he better not make her.

"Slow down, Nat."

"I told you not to call me that."

Lexi shot in front of Natasha and lay down.

Natasha barely had time to sidestep to keep from falling over the dog. "Lexi," she snapped, glaring at her partner.

Lexi stood. *"Woof. Woof. Woof."*

"Nat." Ian widened his stance. "Stop. You're not listening."

"He will not get away again." The red taillights on the ATV mocked her, proving she was a failure. She hadn't stopped him in Philadelphia and she hadn't caught him here. No more. He wasn't claiming another victim. This ended today.

Her boots splashed mud with her march. "I will get him." She glared at Ian. "Do you hear me? I. Will. Not. Lose."

"Nat—"

"If you call me that one more time..." she raged, shaking at the fury singeing her blood.

"Woof. Woof. Woof." Lexi darted between Natasha and Ian and dropped to her stomach again.

"Lexi!" Natasha threw the sign out for the dog to heel.

The German shepherd squirmed but didn't rise.

"Stop." Ian's boots ground into the slop as he stomped toward Natasha.

"No." Her eyes narrowed. "I'm going in there and reclaiming my phone."

"No, you're not." He vaulted over her obstinate dog.

Natasha had just enough time to take a step before Ian wrapped his arms around her and plastered his chest against her back.

"Let. Me. Go." She wiggled and twisted. Her broken body wailed. She refused to give up.

"Nat, stop." Ian's hold tightened. "Stop."

"Never." She bucked, blinking at the spots in her vision. "He can't escape. Don't you get that?"

She connected with his shin.

Ian grunted and lifted her off her feet.

"I won't let him win."

She screamed, the agony from her shoulder becoming too much.

Ian set her down but didn't break his hold.

"I *have* to catch him." Her voice barely held a sound, her throat so torn and raw. "I have to catch him."

"This is not justice," Ian lashed out next to her ear. "This is vengeance."

"No." She rejected the accusation. "Randy killed people. He has to be caught."

"Yes, but not like this. Revenge is not justice."

"Let go of me." She jabbed her hips backward.

Ian dodged.

"I need the phone—"

"Do you want to set off another trap?"

"It's inside—"

"*Look* at your dog." He turned them to face the disguised cabin again. "She's trying to talk to you. She's telling you it's not safe."

Natasha's gaze zeroed in on the solid wood door flapping in the constant wind. It taunted her, beckoning her.

"Do you want to succeed in killing Lexi?"

Ian's words ripped through the door's hypnotic hold. "What?"

"You walk through that door and you kill her," Ian growled. "You'll set off whatever bomb's waiting inside. You'll kill yourself, me, and your dog."

Natasha froze, then lowered her gaze to Lexi, still on her belly. The German shepherd's big brown eyes pleaded with Natasha to listen.

The rage drained, and her soul shattered with it. What had she been about to do?

No answer came, just all-encompassing darkness as she passed out.

Ian blew out a breath at Natasha's sudden unconscious weight filling his arms. "Nat?"

No answer.

Lexi whined, slowly rising. She gazed at her owner, then at Ian.

"She's going to be fine." He had no clue if he'd just lied, but he needed to hear it regardless. She had to be fine. He couldn't handle anything less.

Natasha began to slide down, and his knees started to buckle. "No, you don't." Shifting her weight on his aching ribs, he quickly slid his arm beneath her knees. Muscling her upward, he cradled her close, unable to look away from her face. Less than a minute ago, she was full of fire and fury, ready to battle. Now she seemed diminished. As if more than the fight had drained from her. Something vital had just happened.

"God," he hesitantly whispered, desperate to do something. Terror dripped into his cells, and he'd do anything, including turning to God, to help her. "Please, don't tune me out. I need You. *Please*. Tell me what to do."

A sense of warmth he hadn't experienced in a long time soothed the jagged panic. Ian closed his eyes and lifted his face to the sky. "God? Do You hear me? Please. Show me how to help her."

The overwhelming urge to go back to his Cessna swamped him. Lowering his head, he exhaled, "Thank You."

Lexi pressed her big body against his as if giving and needing the contact.

"We can do this." A lump formed in his throat. He wished he could pet the dog, but his hands were too full. He'd never thought about owning a dog before, but after his experience with Lexi, he couldn't imagine life without a companion. No. That wasn't quite right. No other dog would be this highly trained, extremely intelligent, and loyal. He wanted *Lexi* in his life.

That realization came with sticky issues. In order to have Lexi, he had to be completely open with Natasha. A woman who didn't know about the threat of an arrest hanging over his head. A woman who hadn't given a single indication she saw him as a partner.

He began the long trek back to the plane with precious cargo in his arms, following the dog to keep from stepping on deadly mines.

"Lexi?" he asked, once he put a healthy distance between them and the hideout.

The dog stopped to glance back.

"Is your owner seeing anyone?"

Lexi blinked, then began walking again.

"What does that mean?"

Her tail swished as she kept on going.

"Is she single or not? One nod, yes. Two nods, no."

Nothing.

Figured. The dog could do so many amazing things, he'd hoped understanding English was one of them.

Settling into a steady pace, he contemplated what life could be like with the fiery and dynamic officer Natasha Greene. If he had the guts to confess his past. And if she had the ability to accept it.

Chapter Twenty-Seven

An acrid, chemical odor hit Randy's nose at the same time he realized the engine's intense heat almost cooked his calves. Letting off the gas, Randy drifted to a stop at the edge of an overgrown clearing.

Bending to inspect the visible parts of the motor below his seat, he scrunched his nostrils. Burnt oil overwhelmed the air, and now that he wasn't moving, smoke rose to catch in the wind.

Jumping off, he kicked a heavily treaded tire. *Penny-pinching Russians.* Their outdated everything had made this entire venture miserable.

He stalked a foot into the clearing, the mass of vegetation swallowing the lower half of his legs. Another gust slapped him. Ugh. The oil scent covered him.

Where was Pasha and the rest of his gang?

Randy had been steadily falling behind, and now he understood why. Thanks to the lack of maintenance on the ATV, he was going to miss the plane if someone didn't pick him up.

"Great," he growled, scanning the opposite tree line. Pasha hadn't bothered to pass on the updated landing co-ordinates. He couldn't even attempt to walk to the rendezvous.

The rev of an engine snapped his attention to the left. In moments, Pasha smashed through thick scrubs as he skirted the clearing.

Randy waved his arm, relieved the Russians hadn't abandoned him.

Pasha fumbled with something at his waist as he charged closer. "Debt paid," he yelled as he lifted a Makarov pistol.

Randy threw himself sideways, landing on his stomach. *Crack.* The gunfire echoed.

Randy began commando crawling, using the wild flora to hide.

Traitorous scum. He'd make sure they paid for this.

As soon as he found a way to call his father.

Something hard digging into Natasha's back jolted her awake. Lethargy sat in her chest like an anvil, sapping her will to investigate the lump. Her eyelids felt cemented shut and she didn't care. Easier to hide from the world when she couldn't see it.

The emptiness deep inside grew, encompassing every cell. It drowned her fractured and broken bones, throbbing in agony. It smothered her will to escape the untamed wilderness. And it quelled her endurance to keep going, keep fighting.

She'd failed.

A pang sliced her bleating heart.

She had lost sight of the true meaning of wearing a badge. Catching criminals was not personal. Should *never* become personal. And it had. Somewhere in her planning, she should've recognized the signs, but she hadn't. That was a red flag by itself. The second warning was not telling her shrink about her obsession at their session three days ago. Natasha may not have known the lieutenant's decision to dismiss her informant's lead, but she knew she'd do something herself if she had to.

Her judgment was compromised. If she couldn't trust herself, how could she ask the citizens of Philadelphia to put their faith in her?

The emptiness thickened, driving the air from her lungs as the anvil grew in size.

"Please wake up." A calloused finger brushed her cheek.

She remained still. Interacting took a level of energy she didn't possess.

"Nat." The finger continued to stroke her skin. That annoying nickname. Her brothers tormented her with it all through childhood. Now…despite what she'd yelled before, she'd come to cherish it from Ian. But it still wasn't enough to tempt her to engage.

"Open your eyes. You're scaring me." Clothing rustled and she sensed Ian settling next to her hip. "You've been out for an hour. I don't know what to do."

She didn't either and didn't care. What was the point of tromping through the forest? They were stranded. The closest village was over fifty miles away. In her condition, that might as well be a million. She couldn't trek that. Not to mention their lack of supplies. No water. No food. No means to hunt. Six bullets in a powerful revolver protected them from wolves, but nothing bigger. They'd be bear food by nightfall.

"Hey," he whispered, and puffs of breath hit her chin. "You know I'm desperate if I prayed. Wake up so I can tell you about it." The heat of him dissipated as he shifted back.

She missed his warmth.

"It's been so long, I forgot what to do," he continued rambling. "I asked out loud. I think He heard me. You'd know better though."

She hadn't prayed at all. Ian had done a lot better than her. God had left her. Just like Ian claimed.

Or, her conscience countered, *you ignored the warnings to stop. You interpreted them as obstacles to overcome.*

Just another failure to add to the list. She misunderstood God and His signs. Why bother praying if she wasn't going to comprehend His answers?

"Nat," Ian interrupted again. "Lexi is getting tired of me asking her questions."

The name of her partner shriveled Natasha's battered heart. The German shepherd deserved someone better. Someone who pampered her for the years of exemplary service. The dog should be basking in retirement, not trotting through Alaskan forests, searching for bombs. She should be snoring in her bed, not stranded with a pair of humans who had no way to call for help.

The fresh, phantom slices through Natasha's heart had her gasping. Rolling to her side, she bumped into Ian's knee. A sob wrenched from her soul and she curled against the pain bubbling upward.

"I almost killed her." The words tore out of Natasha's reinjured throat. Uncaring if it made her look weak, she shifted to lie on Ian's thigh.

Ian scooped her up and cradled her.

She buried her face in his coat, unable to hold back. For the second time, she fell apart in his arms.

He just held her. He didn't offer meaningless platitudes or try to convince her everything was okay. His silence was exactly what she wanted and needed.

Her therapist had been right. Her rational thinking had been affected by the vestibule trap. More than Natasha realized or comprehended until now.

"I'd offer you a wrinkled napkin," Ian's deep voice eventually rumbled against her ear. "But I ran out. And I'm not sure they'd have survived the sleet anyway."

Her nose really did need attention, but her breaking heart didn't care about runny grossness.

"Want to know how my plane ended up hosting a juice party?"

Not really, but she nodded. She didn't care what he talked about as long as she didn't have to participate.

"I got a call that a grandfather and grandson needed to fly to Brenbrook."

She had no idea where Brenbrook was located.

"My morning was open, so I agreed to pick them up and take them." Ian smoothed a piece of hair off her forehead. He must've taken his hat back, but she didn't want to open her eyes to find out.

His story continued with the grandfather attending an impromptu summer party thrown by the grandfather's two daughters—one, the boy's mother. The grandfather was in charge of bringing the drink. Apparently, the old man was famous for his homemade juice made from local berries.

She pictured Ian trying to talk the old man into securing the beverage cooler and backing down when the grandfather refused to listen. The turbulence causing the juice to splash everywhere, including the boy, teased a silent chuckle inside Natasha.

"I won't make that mistake again—"

His words cut off.

Pieces of her heart bleated for him. "I'm sorry," she rasped.

He sighed. "I am too."

"I should've been honest from the beginning." Guilt and remorse added their weight onto the anvil crushing her. "If I had told you I was a police officer after a criminal, you probably would've turned me down. You wouldn't have lost your plane."

"I doubt I would've turned you down." Tension grew in his muscles. "I've only rejected a few fares since I moved here."

The emptiness refused to loosen its grip, but she managed to tap into a speck of curiosity. "What happened five months ago?"

His muscles hardened.

At the continued silence, she cracked the seals securing her heavy eyelids. Shifting her head, she peered at his face. Air began drying her ugly-cry skin. His beard hid his jaw but not the muscle ticking near his ear.

She didn't have the energy to push for an answer. Her lids had begun to shut when he spoke.

"My fiancée broke off our engagement."

The flat statement stunned her. "You were engaged?"

"You don't have so sound so shocked." His beautiful eyes met hers. "Is it so outlandish a woman agreed to marry me?"

Heat engulfed her cheeks. "No," she blurted. "It's just I can't imagine you settling down."

"Ouch."

The anvil grew heavier. She couldn't say or do anything right. "I'm making it worse."

"You sure are."

"Hey." Her eyelids popped fully open. "Was she a pilot like you?" The woman had to be an adventurer or something equally rugged to keep up with a bush pilot.

The mirth fizzled in his irises. "No." He paused as if deliberating, then continued, "She was a marketing VP for a large consulting firm. Not sure how I got her attention—"

Natasha knew. Snatches of charming vitality had poked through at times. Like now.

"—in the bookstore but she agreed to go on a date. Seven months later, we were engaged."

"Bookstore?" The hoarse question slipped out.

"Now you think I can't read?" His pale eyes narrowed. "Exactly how low on the human scale am I in your mind?"

"Not low at all." Another response she hadn't expected to utter.

His eyelids widened and a slow grin spread across his lips. "Really," he drew out. "That sounds promising."

"Depends on what you're angling for." What was going on with her mouth? Depression had its fist squeezing her chest to the point she could barely breathe, yet her mouth carried on a conversation beyond her capabilities.

"A date."

She blinked at his instant response. "A date?"

"Again with the shock. My ego can't survive a conversation with you."

"I think your ego is healthy enough for a few jabs."

He laughed. The deep, rich sound echoed. She snuggled her cheek against his chest to feel the vibrations.

Chapter Twenty-Eight

❧

"*Woof. Woof.*" Lexi poked her nose against Natasha's exposed cheek.

"Hey, girl." Natasha's heart thumped as a new round of phantom slices cut into the organ. "I'm sorry."

Lexi licked her cheek.

Natasha dismissed the affection. She had almost killed… A lump formed in her throat, and the anvil pressing on her gained another layer of weight.

"You should thank her."

Ian's announcement slowed her spiraling thoughts.

"Why?" she rasped, keeping her eyes closed to block out her partner. Shame wouldn't allow her to hold Lexi's gaze. "What'd she do?"

"She led us through the buried bombs and back to the plane." Pride laced the words. Lexi licked her cheek again, demanding attention.

Cracking her eyes, the blurry image of a panting German shepherd filled Natasha's sight. "Thank you, sweetheart."

"Hey," Ian rumbled. "I'm a sweetheart too. I *carried* you."

It finally sunk in that Ian was purposefully teasing her and drawing her into conversation. She must have really scared him when she remained unconscious, or he sensed her despondency and wanted to battle it. Maybe both.

Her mind wasn't up to producing witty comebacks, so she voiced the first thing that popped in. "Don't Neanderthals always haul their women from place to place?"

"First off." He unwound his arm from her knees. Her legs rested on top of his thigh as her boots gently hit the ground. "You said I wasn't that low on the human scale." He pointed at her. "Secondly, are you admitting you're *my* woman? Did we just skip dating?" He stroked his beard. "I'm not sure how I feel about that. On the one hand, it saves a lot of money and time, *but* then I miss out on learning all your quirks."

He swiped his hand in the air. "Nope. I've decided," he announced dramatically. "I reject your cavewoman claim on me. You'll have to woo me like all the other women who have tried in the past."

She blinked. The hold on her chest eased. The depression still had its grip, but it wasn't strangling her anymore. Her injuries, on the other hand, were an entirely different matter.

"Nice try," she pushed past her sore throat. Then a new thought sliced through the heaviness. Had he picked up on her growing feelings? Did he know how much her soul yearned to stay connected to him? She'd have no problem wooing him…once she understood what he hid.

"Nice try?" He gazed at her with faux innocence. "I have no idea what you mean. You're the one who took my probing for a date to the college level. *You* called yourself my woman. *I* didn't."

Embarrassed she'd inadvertently announced her interest, she switched topics. His shaggy hair was wet, and somehow, he'd lost the mud and dirt previously coating him. "How are you so clean?" Her tongue searched for any hint of moisture. "Did you find water?"

Every organ inside cried for the sustenance. Her chapped lips puckered and she tried to swallow, with no success.

"Changing the topic, huh?" His eyes twinkled. "I'll allow it. For now." He stroked his cleaner beard. "I didn't want to leave you alone, so I washed up in the stream below." He pointed.

She blinked, only now paying attention to their surroundings. He had carried her back to the ravine, but they remained at the top of the steep hill. Not far below, the Cessna rocked in the tapering wind. The gusts weren't as strong and the clouds weren't as thick. Maybe the storm was finally passing.

Peering down, her tongue throbbed. The clear, rushing water was now twice as deep since they first landed.

"I drank from it too," he announced.

"Is it safe?" She always heard a person couldn't drink directly from streams and rivers. Didn't hikers carry tabs or something to purify water?

He shrugged. "My body didn't care, to be honest."

She understood. She had the urge to fly down the hill and shove her face beneath the surface of the water.

"The stream's been rushing, not stagnant. And I figured we can't get more remote, so it can't be that polluted."

Worked for her. "I want down there." The desert filling her mouth obstructed her tongue from speaking clearly.

Ian gently set her on…a bed of branches?

"Where did these come from?"

"Uh, the trees?" He motioned to the area in general.

She grunted. Stroking green spruce needles, her fingers stuttered on an object. She plucked the pinecone and tossed it at him.

He got the hint to provide a real answer. "The storm flung branches and debris all over the place." He hoisted himself to his feet. "Lexi and I wrestled a few in place so you didn't sleep in the mud."

Her battered heart melted. "Thank you." That was beyond thoughtful and sweet. She had a lot of decisions to make and fallout to face, but there was one thing she didn't have to think twice about—she didn't want to let Ian go.

"Eat these first." He scooped blueberries and red berries from a pile near the bottom of her "bed" into his palms and held them out to her.

Her stomach growled. She clapped a hand over the audible noise. The last time she remembered eating was a quick breakfast at the hotel before she checked out. Wow. Was that really only yesterday morning? So much had happened since then, it felt like a lifetime had passed.

She plucked as many berries as her one hand could hold, then dropped them all in her mouth. The rich, fresh taste exploded on her tongue and the miniscule juice helped coat the inside.

"Eat them all," Ian encouraged, keeping his cupped hands in front of her. "We're surrounded by these."

He didn't have to tell her twice. She finished the pile in seconds.

"I didn't know if Lexi could have them, so I discouraged her from eating them too."

At the mention of Lexi, the dog barked, her brown eyes following Ian's progress from gathering the rest of the pile.

"She's allowed." Natasha greedily snatched more. "They're actually really good for her."

"Sorry, girl." Ian scratched between the dog's ears when one of hands were empty. "I'll pick more just for you. After we get your owner—"

"Partner," Natasha corrected. "Lexi's my partner." The anvil on her chest grew heavy again. "Well, she was. Last week the police station gave her a retirement ceremony."

Natasha's eyes blurred. "She can't physically keep up with her duties anymore."

"I'm sorry." His shoulders drooped.

Natasha nodded. "We both have lung damage, thanks to the chemicals in the foam." She cleared her throat. "Hers is permanent, but mine has a chance of recovering. And you've seen she has trouble with her back leg."

"Do you get to keep her?"

"Yes." She swallowed against the lump rising. "Uh, I guess that does make me her owner now, in the traditional sense, but she's better than a partner. She's family." The corners of her eyes burned. "I don't know what I would've done if the department hadn't gifted her to me. I can't imagine life without her."

The tears she tried to hold back fell anyway. She had come so close to hurting, possibly killing—

She lost the fight to keep the berries in her stomach.

"Nat."

The branch bed jostled as Ian crawled up the middle. She didn't want him witnessing any more of her weakness. He'd seen too much already.

She tried to swat him away, but with one hand, it was virtually impossible. She had to hold herself up and fight her loose hair.

He gathered her locks and she wanted to shout at him to stop being nice. She didn't deserve nice. He should hate her. Lexi should leave her.

Dry heaves stabbed her aching ribs and collarbone.

"Let it out," Ian soothed. "It's obvious you've been holding too much in. It's just us here. Let go."

Chapter Twenty-Nine

Ian carefully wended through the berry bushes, the bottom half of his coat turned upward in a makeshift holder. He'd stuffed as many berries as he could within.

Lexi trailed behind him, gobbling the blue-and-red fruit falling out as he trekked back to Natasha's makeshift bed.

The tenacious woman had passed out not long after throwing up. He probably should've kept her awake, but he didn't have the heart. She had been through a horrific ordeal, then put herself through another one by traveling to Alaska.

Dropping to his knees, he grimaced at the mud saturating his jeans. He doubted he'd wear denim again without thinking about this trip. Same with eating anything containing blue-or-red berries. He'd eaten so many, he couldn't stomach any more, but they were all he could scrounge without abandoning Natasha.

Dribbling a pile for Lexi at the bottom of Natasha's bed, he motioned for the dog to dig in. Lexi didn't hesitate. The berries were gone in seconds and she eyed his jacket for more. Softly chuckling, he doled out another pile.

"Save some for me," a hoarse, sleepy voice called.

He snapped his attention to Natasha, finding her red,

swollen eyes staring at the bottom of his coat. "Come and get it."

He wanted her to move. Too much lying around stiffened muscles and fed into the depression. His mother had battled with the disease all his life. He'd seen the highs and recognized the signs for the lows grabbing hold. Natasha deserved to feel all the emotions she wanted, but he didn't want her trapped inside her head. If hers was anything like his mother's, nasty thoughts and malicious critiques undermined everything.

He had no doubt she'd be back in fighting form in no time. She was the strongest person he'd ever met. He just hoped she took some time to process everything before she jumped back into work.

Taking pity on her pathetic crawling, he met her halfway and sat.

"You ready for a frigid bath?" He made idle conversation while she inhaled the berries.

She shivered. "Not really. But I can't wait to drink. I'm so thirsty."

"Right there with you." He couldn't scoop enough to satisfy his body. "Need a lift?" He held out a hand.

Natasha snorted as her cheeks flared pink. "I'd say I'm not helpless." She picked at the spruce needles. "But I hate that I am."

"Ahhh," he scoffed. "You'll be back to making criminals tremble in no time." He kept his tone light. Now was not the time to dive into anything heavy. They needed a break from this nightmare adventure.

"I don't know." She tapped on a branch. "You're pretty wicked with one of these in your hands. You made that Mafia guy sorry."

Ian winced. "Don't remind me." He blocked the replay trying to flare in his mind.

Warmth from her grip eased the chill on his red skin. "So, what's the plan?"

"For your bath?" He scratched his beard with his free fingers. It needed a razor. "Simple. Haul you down there and drop you in the water."

"Ha. Ha."

He grinned, loving that she responded to his flirting. It had been a long time since he even wanted to flirt. Given the harrowing situation, who knew he'd have the opportunity or a receptive woman?

You should tell her.

He muzzled the little voice in his head. Later. Maybe after she was clean.

The little voice knew it for the lie it was. She looked at him with interest. She flirted back and even agreed to a date, maybe. Why ruin it now with accusations of smuggling?

"I mean," she interrupted the internal battle. "How do we get out of here?"

"Oh." He adjusted the hat on his head. "I'm still working on that."

A spark of life flashed in her hazel eyes. "You don't have *anything* figured out?"

"Normally I give my coordinates to the front desk before every flight." He didn't have a death wish. "It's a way to file a flight plan. Especially when off-airport landings are involved."

"Normally," she repeated, the crease between her eyes deepening. "But not this time?"

"Uh." He scratched the back of his neck. He really didn't want to confess the reason for his lack of intelligence.

"Dalton." Her eyes narrowed. "Why not this time?"

"Uh, oh. You used my last name." He stalled, racking his mind for something, anything other than the real reason.

"Why. Not. This. Time?"

Heat flared over his cheeks. Nothing came to mind. "I was rattled, okay?" He threw his arm away from his neck. "I wasn't thinking clearly. *You*—" he jabbed a finger at her "—put me in some kind of trance the second I walked into the lobby. Made me forget almost everything."

Her jaw dropped and her eyes widened.

He groaned, dropping his face into his hands. *So embarrassing.*

"Really," she drew out, mimicking him from earlier.

He lifted his head, brazening out the blush coating his skin. "Skip had already flown away and Kaya was on the phone." He kept his hands from rubbing his neck again. "None of us realized the oversight."

Lexi's gaze bounced between her humans.

A Cheshire cat smile split Natasha's lips—another to match his from earlier. He shouldn't have teased her. It was now coming back to bite him.

"Ace." She leaned into his space. "Is there anything *else* you'd like to confess? Anything *interesting* I should know?"

Yes, his conscience answered. *Tell her now.* "As a matter of fact there is." He plucked his hat off and smoothed his hand through his damp hair.

Unfiltered curiosity and interest leveled on him.

Words failed to find his tongue. "I'm a smuggler" was not the best opening and wrong on top of that. He wasn't a criminal, but no one believed him. His fiancée left after the first accusation. His father never said he didn't believe Ian, but he never gave any indication he thought his son was innocent either. His uncle put distance between them. When the story broke on the news, he'd lost his job with the construction company. The owner cited reasons for the termination, but really, the guy didn't want any more reporters stalking job sites. The federal task force absolutely thought him guilty. Everyone did. Why wouldn't Natasha? She embraced justice so much, she traveled to Alaska to obtain it.

Innocent people didn't find themselves in the middle of investigations. His ex-fiancée's parting words blasted through his mind, amping the fear.

An insidious voice proclaimed that law enforcement stuck together. That she'd side with the task force.

Moisture fled his mouth. He wasn't ready to lose her yet. For now, he could forget the outside world. Natasha didn't need to know a thing yet. Besides, they were stranded. He had plenty of time to tell her.

Slapping his hat back on his head, he schooled his features with graveness. "I didn't want to say anything before."

Her expression turned wary at his tone.

"But..." He made her wait a few seconds. "You have mud *all over* your face. You really need to—"

A pinecone smacked his chest. A second beaned off his hat.

Lexi hopped to her paws, barking. She wanted in on the fun.

He plucked one of the pinecones off his lap and chucked it at the dog. "You need a bath too. You and you partner are a mess."

A third cone caught him in the cheek. "Hey." He mock glared at Natasha. "I'll dunk you in the water if you keep it up."

"You planned to do that anyway." She eyed him with suspicion, then relaxed. "With the muck all over my pants and coat, I'll probably not retaliate if you do."

He snorted. "That's probably big of you."

She grabbed his hand again. "All righty. Let the glacial bathing begin."

Chapter Thirty

Natasha clamped her left arm around her shins, and hugged tight. She'd be amazed if she didn't shiver right off the boulder.

"That..." Her voice trembled. "W-w-was...be-be-yond-d c-c-cold."

"Woof. Woof. Woof." Lexi splashed through the rushing water, having a grand time.

Ian plopped onto the boulder next to her and shivered. "A-a-gre-greed."

Poor guy. He had waded into the water to help rinse her hair. She had tried by herself, but her right collarbone kept screaming. Thankfully, the cast on her upper arm was waterproof, so it didn't matter if it got wet. And it had. Profusely.

The sun attempted to peek through the gray clouds again and she prayed it stayed for good. She needed warmth.

"D-d-do you—" her body shuddered "—think-k we c-c-can...fire." She gave up trying to speak in sentences. "Fire. N-need."

Ian's mouth tilted down as he studied the landscape. "Wind...died...enough." He crossed his arms, shoving his red, raw hands beneath the sleeves of his coat. "No... m-matches."

"L-l-lighter." It took all her willpower to point to a side pocket on her pants. "S-stole."

"Of-ficer…an-and thief. C-cool." He tilted his head. "It wo-work? W-was in wa-water."

Her grin almost cracked her lips. "He…had pri-priorities." She waited out a tremor. "Water…proof li-lighter. But. Inappropriate…clo-clothing."

Ian snorted.

The only good thing she could say about the frigidity of the water was her body had just had an ice bath. Her sore muscles were shocked into temporary pain relief. Whether she developed pneumonia was a worry for later.

"I—I'll…g-gather…wood." Ian didn't move. "In a…in a…minute."

She understood. Everything, from her hair to her toes, was soaked. Her clothing was plastered to her, pressing the cold against her. It was a wonder icicles didn't form. Every breeze and wind gust drove the chill in deeper.

Not all the mud scrubbed off her pants, but they were a lot better than before. Same with her skin. She felt so much cleaner and awake.

Lexi stopped jumping and snapped her head up.

Natasha followed her partner's line of sight to the northwest. The midmorning sun pierced her eyes, disorienting her.

"What's…?" Ian also gazed upward. "Someone's coming."

Natasha squinted and blinked, trying to clear the spots from her vision. "T-toward us?" Hope swelled and she wanted to bounce. They were saved.

He lifted a hand, shielding his eyes. "I think so."

She copied his stance, straining to see. The speck grew larger. "Is there—" she blinked against the sun "—m-more than o-one?"

He leaned forward, not answering.

Giddiness washed out the anxious dread, thawing her blood. "Search and rescue?" *Thank You, Lord. We're saved.*

Scanning the sky again, she blinked at another growing specter, this one coming from the south. "Ian." She knocked his boot with hers. "Look."

He twisted. "Why would someone be flying from that direction?"

"I don't care." She kept her attention on the south. "As long as they pick us up and take us to civilization, I'm good with wherever they started."

One black object turned into two, then three.

"How many do you count?" she asked, her neck kinking.

"Four."

That wasn't right. Search and rescue didn't need that many for two stranded people. Even with SAR not knowing her and Ian's conditions, they wouldn't have the budget to activate that many personnel and equipment.

"Something's wrong," she murmured, the hope deflating into unease. "Lexi, heel."

The dog splashed through the water, then onto the rocky shore. She trotted to the boulder and stationed herself beside it.

The buzzing in the sky grew louder. In moments, it thundered and echoed off the land and trees.

Helicopters. All of them. Not a single plane charged toward them.

"Nat?" Ian's uncertainty bled through that one syllable. "What's going on?"

The sleek underbody of a Sikorsky Black Hawk roared directly overhead, drowning out everything.

A second Black Hawk split to the right, while a tactically enhanced Bell veered left. No identification was painted on the bottom of any, except for a series of numbers on the Bell.

The one from the north joined the other three, with TROOPERS in white letters stamped on the blue bottom.

"Natasha?" Ian shouted above the pounding noise. "Talk to me."

"Maybe they received a tip about Randy Puckett." It was the only thing that made sense, but who would do that? Only Natasha believed her informant and she hadn't told the Alaska State Troopers or the FBI she was in the area, investigating. Unsanctioned. On her own. A no-no she had hoped to get away with. Her initial plan had her calling them in for the arrest, but the plane wreck changed everything.

Three of the helicopters circled low with her, Ian, and Lexi in the center. The first Black Hawk roared back overhead with both side doors opened. It paused yards away, spinning in its hover to face them. The main rotor diameter prevented the Sikorsky from fitting between the two steep hills to land; it was a lot wider than the Cessna's wingspan.

The rotor wash from the whirling blades tried to blast her off the boulder. Dirt and small debris soared, pinging and smacking into everything.

She slapped her eyes closed and wished she had earplugs. Constant ringing was going to fill her hearing soon.

Splashing and thudding had her squinting with her hand near her face. Ropes. Thick ropes still connected to the Black Hawk thumped into the water and rock bed.

Multiple helmeted heads wearing goggles peered down and her stomach plunged. "This isn't search and rescue."

"What?"

Ian barely got the question out when a unit of men and women fast-roped out of the helicopter. Their boots hit the ground in seconds.

"Woof. Woof. Woof. Woof." Lexi continuously barked, standing in front of the boulder.

A chorus of "Raise your hands" hit Natasha as the tactical unit situated their black M4 carbine assault rifles on them. Dressed in fatigues, gloves, full Kevlar protection with FBI emblazoned on the chest and sleeves, they meant business.

What was going on?

The Black Hawk lifted and veered away, joining the circling birds. The unrelenting gusts dissipated, leaving the remaining debris to drift in little tornados.

"Raise your hands" barraged her and Ian again.

Lexi barked, her growl warning the newcomers to back away.

The tactical team—most likely SWAT—didn't heed her threat.

Natasha lifted her only good hand in surrender. "I'm a police officer," she shouted above the chaos, pushing her painful throat to utter the words. "Lexi is my K-9. She's trained—" Her voice gave out and she hacked.

"Don't move" was the only response. The unit fanned out, aiming their carbines with practiced precision.

The second Black Hawk broke from the circle and lowered to hover at the top of the steep hill, yards from the edge. A fresh round of wind from the blades knocked into her, agitating the debris. Oversize, black, military-grade containers were lowered out of both sides. Her angle prevented her from seeing them touch the ground, but it didn't matter. More supplies kept joining the others.

When the helicopter veered away, Natasha focused on the unit in front of them. "What's going on?" she rasped, wincing at the pain.

Chapter Thirty-One

"Keep your hands up and don't move," a male voice barked from the center of the group.

Natasha scanned the bristling tactical unit. Most wore body cameras on their Kevlar vests. Dread pumped through her blood alongside a healthy dose of anger. Instead of search and rescue, someone had activated SWAT. That same someone wanted the entire exchange recorded, and there was only one real reason for that. She and Ian weren't being saved, they were being detained, maybe even arrested, and the digital footage could be used as evidence in court.

What. Was. Going. On?

The tall man in the center signaled to the man on the right end.

A truncated animal-control pole appeared from inside the guy's vest.

Fire blasted through Natasha's veins. Lexi didn't deserve to be manhandled. She was a hero who'd almost died trying to capture a criminal. They should be tossing her treats, not threatening her.

Lexi lowered her head and growled.

"Lexi." Natasha fought to speak, her throat too sore to produce much sound. "Silence. Heel." It hurt to give the commands, but Lexi could be seriously injured if she put up a fight.

The German shepherd hushed immediately and hobbled backward to Natasha.

Natasha exhaled. The dog may be trained, but she wasn't mindless. Lexi could decide to ignore Natasha and attack.

The man pulled on the aluminum to extend the pole to its full length. Once he had maximum reach, he fed the cable over Lexi's head.

Lexi jerked against the device, but the man was quicker, locking the cable in place and holding on.

Natasha swallowed against the emotions clogging her airway. "Lexi," she pleaded. "Don't fight."

SWAT didn't care about Lexi's pedigree or training, they cared about securing the scene. Everyone going home safely at the end of the day was always the priority. And Lexi presented an unknown danger to these men and women.

But that didn't mean Natasha couldn't ratchet down the tension. Shifting her focus to the guy controlling the pole, she asked, "Do you have a muzzle?" She cleared her torn throat. "I'll put it on for you."

The guy looked to the tall man in the center. Tall Leader jerked his chin to the man closest to Control Pole Guy. That man lowered his carbine and closed the distance to his teammate.

"Left side pocket." CPG slid a leg outward.

The man plucked out a soft, black, neoprene device and marched toward Natasha.

Lexi growled.

The man stopped.

"Lexi, heel." Natasha prayed the German shepherd listened. She didn't want this situation to escalate.

Lexi quieted but didn't remove her gaze from the man.

"I'm going to stand," Natasha announced to keep itchy fingers off triggers.

"I can help," Ian offered.

"It's best if you don't." Natasha pushed off the boulder. She slowly met the man at the edge of the rushing water.

Taking the muzzle, she studied the mechanics and understood how it worked. The padded loop that went over the snout had Velcro to ensure a tight fit so the dog couldn't open her mouth. Then a set of straps locked behind the dog's head to keep Lexi from shaking the loop off. Simple, humane, and effective.

Lexi didn't fight Natasha applying the muzzle. Her brown eyes were full of confusion, but she trusted Natasha enough to become vulnerable.

Kissing her partner's snout, Natasha straightened and turned to Tall Leader. "I suppose you're going to frisk us next?"

"Yes." Tall Leader gave another signal.

While CPG led Lexi away, a man and a woman broke formation. Gravel and rocks crunched under their boots as each headed forward, the man to Ian, the woman to Natasha.

"This is normal, Ian." Natasha shifted enough to keep him in sight.

Ian looked ready to pass out. Pale green eyes tracked to her and he visibly swallowed.

The next twenty minutes were full of invasive inspections. The first round relieved Ian of his revolver and found no weapons on Natasha. The second round had the paramedic within SWAT medically assess her and Ian. The woman prodded and poked, tsking under her breath periodically. She asked a slew of questions, confirming their identity as well as other basic information to assess their cognitive levels. Verdict: they weren't in a coma and would live.

Yay. Natasha's body dreamed of dropping into one to get some rest.

The only good part about the examination was the bottle of water and power bar. The woman barely had them in her hands when Ian snatched them and handed Natasha her set.

The paramedic faced Tall Leader as she snapped off her nitrile gloves. "They're dehydrated, and I'm 99 percent sure concussed. They should be checked out at a hospital."

Yep. Natasha greedily gulped the last of the water. She and Ian had survived a plane crash. They absolutely needed a hospital.

"Can they answer questions?" Tall Leader asked flatly, no compassion in sight.

"Yes." The paramedic tossed the gloves into her bag.

"Then, there's no rush."

"Yes, sir." The woman collected the empty water bottles and wrappers, then melted back in with the unit.

Natasha wanted to toss something at Tall Leader's head. She needed more water and food. Now. But it was useless to make demands. The SWAT leader was following a specific set of orders.

"I'm not answering anything—" she lifted her chin "—until I meet the incident commander."

Ian tried to block the chaos roaring all around him, but it drilled into his psyche. The day he'd been dreading for five months had finally arrived.

His stomach plunged.

Jail. He was going to jail.

For too many seconds, his mind blitzed, unable to comprehend the sudden change in his future.

He'd never be free. Never soar the skies again. Never get married and have a family… His eyes strayed to Natasha, standing like a general between him and the tall guy in charge. She didn't know she was fighting on the wrong side. He should've told her, but he thought he had more time.

Jail. The word caught in his throat. Conflicting messages confused his body's responses: Run. Stay. Cry. Rage. Cower. Cooperate.

Tall Guy swirled a closed fist deliberately overhead.

The smaller Bell helicopter zipped downward from circling. The pilot expertly maneuvered the aircraft between the steep hills, behind the tactical arc of FBI agents. The main rotor diameter was about the same length as Ian's forlorn Cessna's wingspan, allowing the pilot to set the bird on the rock bed unlike the Black Hawk. The blades remained spinning, broadcasting the Bell wasn't sticking around.

Gusts raged across the open space, kicking up dirt and debris. Ian should've saved himself the painful ice bath. He'd need another one by the time the helicopters finished their parade of drop-offs.

He inwardly snorted. Fanciful wishing. He wouldn't have a chance to do anything except wear handcuffs and head to jail.

The copilot's door unlatched and the occupant fought against the gusting wind to open it.

The SWAT member beside Tall Guy broke from formation to grab the door. He held it open while a man stepped on the rungs, then jumped to the rock bed.

Worn denim jeans and rugged boots were topped by a green insulated coat ending at his waist. The sides flapped in the unrelenting air and he fought to zip them closed. On one side of his belt was a holstered handgun, and the other had a cell phone in a rugged case. His short black hair whipped wildly as he squinted against the cloud of grit.

The pilot smoothly lifted the Bell straight up. Once he reached open air, he veered toward the south and raced away from the scene.

The way the mid-thirties newcomer strode with authority announced that he was in charge.

Marching forward, escorted by the FBI guy in full gear, Newcomer fiddled with a length of bead chain around his neck until a shiny gold badge rested on the front of his coat.

Tall Guy shifted sideways to greet Newcomer. The underdressed man flattened his wayward hair as they exchanged a few words. Tall Guy motioned to Ian and Natasha. Newcomer glanced their way, then nodded.

With three helicopters still circling, Ian had no hope of overhearing the low conversation. Whatever they talked about kept their faces grim. Not that any of this was a joyous occasion. At least for him, Natasha, and poor Lexi.

The German shepherd stood beside the steep hill. The FBI guy still held the pole thing Ian had seen dogcatchers use in cartoons to nab strays. The muzzle prevented Lexi from biting and barking, and Ian bet she wanted to do both.

Natasha shifted, then slowly ambled backward to the boulder. Why had the FBI targeted her? She had nothing to do with his supposed smuggling. Could it be a misunderstanding? A blip of hope rose, then fell. No. If the FBI wanted her, assault rifles wouldn't target him.

Nothing made sense.

His entire future hung in the balance and he was helpless to do anything but wait for the verdict.

Chapter Thirty-Two

Ian swiped a trembling palm over his face. Every second lasted an hour and he couldn't take the suspense anymore.

Tall Guy touched the strap around his throat. His lips moved, but Ian couldn't read what they said.

"Watch what you say," Natasha rasped, standing next to him. "You hear me?"

Ian nodded and repeated, "Watch what I say."

Her body shivered; her clothes and hair were still wet. "See those cameras on their vests?"

He scanned the men and women staring at them. Oh. He saw them now.

"They're recording," she explained.

Oh, God, he prayed. *Please. I need Your help. What do I do? Is there a way to stop the arrest? I'm begging You to convince the FBI I'm innocent.* His breath caught at the mental images of cuffs and Natasha turning away from him. *I don't want to lose her, Lord. Please. Help me.* Life had become surreal and he wanted to wake up. Now.

The badge swung with Newcomer's movement as he turned their way and closed the distance. Loose rocks forced him to zigzag, but he swerved with swagger.

This guy knew he was the top dog.

The FBI SWAT leader marched a step behind, his boots crushing stones underfoot.

The rest of the tactical team adjusted positions to keep Ian and Natasha in their sights.

Tight lines formed at the corners of Newcomer's mouth and he gave off the vibe of coiled intensity. Weren't FBI agents supposed to be in suits? Movies and TV didn't always emulate life, but he couldn't wipe the image from his mind.

"I'm Rich Worthington," Newcomer announced, his voice raised above the roaring overhead. "I'm an ASAC in the FBI's Anchorage field office."

ASAC? Ian had heard the term but couldn't remember what it stood for. Right now, he'd be amazed if he remembered his name, his nerves were strung so tight.

"I'm assuming you're responsible for activating SWAT?" Natasha asked, her raspy voice flat.

"What's an ASAC?" Ian blurted, his anxiety controlling his mouth instead of his brain.

"Assistant special agent in charge," Rich answered, flicking a glance at Ian, then held Natasha's bold stare. "Yes. I called in SWAT."

"Why?" Natasha challenged, not backing down.

Ian admired the woman, unfazed by the ASAC's authoritative demeanor or the fact the guy had the power to arrest her. Not to mention the hulk towering over all of them could crush her with his fist.

"This is Special Agent Doyle." Worthington motioned to the hulk. "He's the operations commander."

Doyle didn't twitch or offer a hint of a smile. He kept his gun angled toward the ground, but his finger near the trigger. The round camera lens on the man's vest had a perfect shot of Ian and Natasha.

"Where is Randy Puckett?" Rich was obviously finished with pleasantries.

Natasha's chin snapped back. "How did you know Puckett was here?"

"*Was* here?" Rich frowned. "Where is he now?"

"Gone."

The crease between Rich's brows deepened. "Where?"

"That way." Natasha pointed toward the east. "He and his buddies took off on four-wheelers."

"Why did they leave you and Mr. Dalton behind?"

Ian jerked. "What?" *Leave us behind?*

Rich didn't react to Ian's question. "You two are still here. Why?"

"Wait a minute." Thunderclouds stormed Natasha's expression. "Let me see if I understand correctly. You believe Ian and I *met* with Randy Puckett?"

"What?" Ian asked again, floored by the sudden turn in direction. "I thought you were here about smuggling." The words dropped in the space like a cement ball. He wanted to kick himself. *Why* had he asked that out loud?

"Smuggling?" Natasha parroted. Blazing hazel eyes burned him at the same time Rich answered, "We'll get to that in a minute."

Everything seized. Ian couldn't blink, breathe, or think. That statement meant the beginning of the end of his freedom. Of his life. Of everything.

"No." Natasha held up her left hand. "We'll get to that now. *What* smuggling, Ian?"

"Officer Greene," Rich lashed, standing straighter. He now beat Ian's height by a few inches. "*I'll* ask the questions."

"Am I under arrest?" she countered.

"There are issues that need resolving," Worthington countered.

She flattened her mouth. "Am. I. Free. To. Leave?"

Rich smirked. "By all means." He swiped a hand at the

rushing water and the other steep hill. "Feel free to hike anywhere you want."

Lightning flashed in her irises to go with the storm on her face.

"But, if you answer my questions," Rich continued, his tone just shy of mocking, "I'd be happy to fly you and Mr. Dalton to the hospital."

"After the interrogation." Natasha's skin whitened on her left clenched fist.

"Conversation. Interrogation." Rich shrugged. "Where did Randy Puckett go?"

"I already told you." Natasha growl-sighed. "That way." She pointed again.

"Doyle." Rich split his attention between Natasha and the hulk. "Send the other team east."

Doyle focused on Natasha, then Ian. "Any particular region?"

Natasha shrugged. "Don't know."

"They didn't exactly give us an itinerary when they took off," Ian spit out, the agitation and anxiety controlling his mouth again.

"What 'exactly' *did* they give you?" Rich pounced, boring his dark brown gaze into Ian.

"Uh." He blinked at the ferocity. "Nothing?"

"You sure?" Worthington pressed. "You don't sound—"

"He's sure," Natasha cut in, glaring at Ian, then at Rich. "We've had *no* communication with Randy Puckett."

"Hmm." Rich gave half his attention to the hulk. "Doyle, tell HRT to begin the search. Also, activate the division of forestry. They'll know landing spots for planes wanting to hide their affairs. And see if the state troopers' K-9 and ordnance teams are finally en route."

Ian didn't have to ask about initials this time. *HRT* stood for *Hostage Rescue Team*. A lot of movies portrayed the elite FBI unit.

Doyle dipped his chin. He tapped his throat strap again and began relaying the orders. Moments later, the second Black Hawk peeled away and headed in the indicated direction.

Ian exhaled. Maybe, just maybe, they'd find Randy Puckett and stop believing he and Natasha had anything to do with the criminal. Ian never imagined this, but he wanted to go back to being accused of smuggling. That was a lot less terrifying than supposedly working with a bomb maker.

Too many questions crowded Natasha's thoughts. She needed to remain clearheaded, but too much had happened in the last thirty-something hours.

She wanted to beg Rich for another bottle of water, but she refused to show any sign of weakness. Until she understood why Worthington believed she and Ian were connected to Randy, she wasn't asking for anything. Except, maybe, a lawyer, depending on their "conversation."

Special Agent Doyle motioned deliberately over his head again. He pressed his hand against one of his ears, listening through the earpiece. She longed for a device so she could hear their plans.

The state trooper helicopter broke from circling. The Airbus AStar was identical to the fleet Philadelphia police owned for air support. It even had a similar blue-and-white paint scheme, with minor differences. Only today, she couldn't count on anyone within to be on her side.

The Airbus aimed for the area at the top of the steep hill, yards away from the edge. Probably close to the equipment cases. It slowly dropped lower, sending another round of air blasting everything.

She shielded her eyes and squinted.

Unlike the Black Hawks, the doors on both sides were

closed. She didn't have the right angle to peer in the windows before it lowered out of sight.

Less than a minute later, the Airbus peeled away, taking its gusts with it. It flew north while the remaining Black Hawk headed south.

The sudden departure left her ears ringing. The constant rumbling of rotor blades pounding against the landscape had dulled her hearing for who knew how long. *Great.* As if she didn't have enough injuries to deal with.

She glanced at Lexi. Her partner had managed to place two paws on the steep hill, near a tall willow thicket, looking upward. Natasha bet she kept fighting the muzzle, trying to bark. Phantom slices cut through her heart at her best friend being treated like a rabid animal.

Latching her glare on to Assistant Special Agent in Charge, Rich Worthington, Natasha thrust her shoulders back. It was time to understand the game he played.

Chapter Thirty-Three

Ian blinked at the controlled chaos happening in the open space at the top of the ravine. A massive tent had been erected with its front and back flaps tied open. Men and women streamed in and out, carrying various equipment from huge black cases dotting the landscape.

"Command center," Natasha uttered hoarsely, leaning on Ian's arm.

He'd take the contact as long as he could. He should've told her about the smuggling investigation when he had the chance. Fear wasn't a good excuse and now he'd lost the ability to sway her to believe him.

"We'll process the evidence in there." Rich waved at the tent.

"What evidence?" Ian asked. He still didn't understand why the guy thought he and Natasha had a connection to Randy.

Doyle grunted, shifting his weight evenly over his boots. His hand snapped up to his ear. "Forensic team's two minutes out."

Worthington rubbed his palms together. "Excellent. I want to collect as much as possible before the weather wipes anything else away."

"What are you hoping to find?" Natasha asked, her voice barely audible.

"You tell me," Rich countered, lowering his hands.

Natasha sighed. "You're going to find a cleverly disguised, single-story structure less than a mile that way." She jabbed a finger. "You'll also discover a ton of bombs planted in the ground and trip wires all over the place."

Rich leaned forward. "Will we?" A calculating light sparked in his eyes. "So you *have* been to the hideout."

Thunderous rotor blades whirled overhead just as two people strode out of the tent with video cameras in their nitrile-gloved hands. As the latest helicopter began lowering, the camera people disappeared over the edge of the hill.

Documenting his Cessna and crash, Ian assumed. Could he ask for a copy of the video to show the insurance company? He doubted it.

Air blasted everyone and everything. The tent crackled and snapped under the intensity but didn't blow away. Impressive securing.

Ian held the top of his hat and braced his legs.

The helicopter's skids had barely touched the ground when people in various clothing jumped from both open sides. The moment everyone cleared, the helicopter lifted and roared toward the south.

The newcomers joined in with the others, emptying the containers and setting up their lab or command center or whatever in the tent.

Rich blocked Ian's line of sight. "So, you've been to the hideout," he repeated.

The answer seemed really important and that made Ian leery. What didn't he know? He got the feeling he was missing something. Well, he was missing a lot, since he didn't understand all the nuances of law enforcement, but this was something else. Did he need to call his lawyers?

Natasha's shoulder dug into Ian's bicep. "Depends on what you're getting at."

Did Rich hear her? Ian had trouble and he couldn't be much closer.

Rich dropped the pleasant veneer. "This is your last chance to come clean. Tell me about your meeting with Randy Puckett. Once we breach the hideout, it's too late."

Natasha raised her chin. "You step one foot in that place and it'll blow."

"Did you just threaten me, Officer Greene?" The menace in Rich's tone raised the hairs on the back of Ian's neck.

"No." Her voice gave out and she cleared her throat. "Randy rigged it."

"When was that?" Rich asked. "After the meeting?"

Natasha opened her mouth, but nothing came out.

Oh man. She'd lost her voice. He relied on her to do all the talking. His track record with law enforcement was horrendous.

"Mr. Dalton." Rich focused on him. "Answer the questions."

Ian swallowed. "Aftertheplanecrash," flew out of his mouth. He stole a cleansing breath and tried again. "Russian Mafia chased us after we… *I*…crash-landed."

"Russian Mafia," Worthington repeated. "How did you know they're Russian Mafia?"

"Well, um." Apparently, his track record held. He was already off to a bad start. "They sounded Russian? And. Um." He pointed at the woman next to him. "She told me."

"I see." Rich rolled his wrist.

Natasha executed a bunch of complicated signs, but her right hand trapped in the sling made it look awkward.

"I don't know sign language." Rich didn't look impressed, but Ian was. He'd seen her use signs with Lexi, but he hadn't realized she was fluent.

Natasha huffed. "Russians," she wheezed so low Ian barely heard.

Rich and Doyle stepped closer.

She opened her mouth, but again, nothing came out.

Sympathy poked through Ian's nerves at the frustration pouring from Natasha.

"Mr. Dalton." Rich's authoritative tone drained the compassion. "Please, continue."

Sweat pooled under Ian's arms and beneath his hat. "Um. Well. These men with assault rifles—" he hesitantly pointed at Doyle "—like his, came running toward the plane. We hid in the forest, then snuck back."

Ian described how the Russians stole their stuff, including Natasha's satellite phone, and destroyed his radio. They were completely stranded with no way to call for help when they made the decision to find the hideout to reclaim their things—

"Is this when you met with Randy Puckett?" Rich wouldn't leave that question alone.

"We never met with Randy." Ian prayed the man believed him. He hadn't been able to convince anyone of his innocence yet, so he didn't hold out hope.

Skipping over the part where he beat one of the criminals with a branch, he cut to the end. "Natasha used Lexi's detection training to uncover Randy's location. He buried *a lot* of bombs." His words were almost slurring together. He had to slow down. "We made it to the structure, and on the table was our stuff. But right then, ATVs started up. Randy and company drove away. Lexi wouldn't let us enter the hideout—"

"So," Rich interjected. "You're saying you and Officer Greene have never been inside?"

"That's right." Why did he think they had?

"And your belongings were stolen. That's how they ended up in the hideout?"

"Yeah." Again, what was he missing?

"That's interesting."

Rich's tone didn't sound interested. It sounded like he didn't believe a word.

Chapter Thirty-Four

Natasha stiffened at Worthington's response. He had an angle, but she couldn't figure it out.

The ASAC pulled a cell phone from his coat pocket and tapped on the large screen. "My office received this around nine this morning."

Whatever the video contained was important enough for the FBI field office to call Rich in on what had obviously been a day off. He then scrambled to organize SWAT, CSI, K-9s, and the bomb squad, based on the footage.

Her stomach knotted.

Worthington tapped on the phone again and turned it to face her and Ian.

Randy Puckett's face from within the decrepit hideout filled the screen.

Fury sparked and her fists clenched. That smug expression haunted her dreams.

In the background were all of her and Ian's belongings. Dark shadows filled the corners with no speck of sunlight. Randy had filmed before sunrise, then time delayed sending the email.

"Hello, esteemed members of the FBI," Randy oozed from the phone's speaker.

She no longer wondered how the Anchorage office knew Randy was in the area.

"For those who don't know me—" the video continued "—my name is Randy Puckett. I've become quite popular with law enforcement lately, but that's not important. Ian Dalton and Officer Natasha Greene need your attention. My time is limited, so you'll have to look them up yourselves."

The image bobbled as Randy adjusted his arm. "Ian invited me and a few members of the Russian Mafia to meet him in Alaska. He wants to expand his smuggling empire. Take it international—"

"Lies," Ian rumbled, vibrating with fury. "*None* of that is true."

Rich stopped the video.

Natasha's stomach contracted like Ian had punched her in the gut. Smuggling empire? She didn't trust Randy's accusation, but Ian had alluded to an investigation when Rich first arrived.

Her heart panged. Ian had never uttered a word about it, even after she thought they'd grown close. Even when she asked him directly if he had anything to tell her.

"Dalton?" she rasped.

"It's not true." He peered down at her, his green eyes pleading for her to believe him. "I'm *not* a smuggler."

"Are *you*, Officer Greene?" Rich snatched her attention.

"Am I what?" Natasha whispered, the only volume she had left.

"A smuggler," Rich accused, his brown eyes narrowing. "Puckett recorded the inside of your luggage. There are some suspicious components wedged between your belongings. On their own, not dangerous, but put together they build a powerful bomb."

The ground fell from beneath her feet and she stumbled. Ian snapped his hand out to grab her, but she didn't want

anyone touching her. Worthington actually thought she'd
work with that monster? After what Randy had done to
her and Lexi? Never. That part of the recording should've
been easily dismissed as a setup. Why would he entertain
the nonsense?

"I had an enlightening conversation with Lieutenant
Aydem." Rich cocked his head, no doubt for effect.

Her pulse thundered, rushing too much blood to her
head.

"He was quite surprised to hear you traveled to Alaska."
Bet he was.

"It took my analysts minutes to track your flights across
America."

She hadn't hidden her identity, so of course they'd found
the flights.

"Lieutenant Aydem filled me in on your last run-in
with Puckett and your informant's sketchy tip." Rich's lips
puckered in distaste. "An officer defying her superior's
direct orders not to investigate the case doesn't help this
situation."

She refused to flinch.

Rich placed his hands behind his back. "Your sick-time
policy specifically states you're not allowed to leave your
house except under limited conditions. You certainly don't
have the lieutenant's permission to override that rule, so
I asked myself: Why would a woman suddenly disregard
her superior and fly to Alaska, the very same place Ian
Dalton escaped to five months ago? And, wow, Randy
Puckett and Russian Mafia are here too?"

She lifted her chin.

"You can understand why I have questions," Rich
pressed. "Anything you want to say now?"

"You won't find—" her throat gave out and she held
up a finger to ask for a moment "—our…fingerprints…
inside." She motioned to the cell phone screen.

Ian inched closer, the crease between his brows furrowed.

She shot him a warning glare. "You…lied…to me."

Ian's heart shriveled at those four words.

Rich's eyes sharpened. "What do you mean by that, Officer Greene?"

Dark hazel irises flashed, then the fire banked as a stony expression filled Natasha's face.

"Nat—"

"Lying by omission is still lying," Natasha cut him off to state to the FBI agent.

Ian cringed. She threw his accusation back at him, word for word.

"Wouldn't you agree, ASAC Worthington?"

Rich flitted his focus between Ian and Natasha. "Yes."

Everything was spiraling out of control. The sledgehammer kept swinging at his life. He hadn't meant to lie.

Yes, you did, his conscience retorted. *She asked if you had anything else to tell her and you made a joke.*

I did and it was foolish. Beyond the shock, did she believe he was a *smuggler*? That he owned an empire? Not for one second did he accept she smuggled pieces of a bomb in her luggage. It didn't matter that she had defied her lieutenant. Rightly so, as it turned out. Randy planted that stuff from his own supply. Ian was sure of it. Would she reject the accusations against him as easily?

He needed a chance to explain.

Doyle pressed his hand against the ear with the black device. "Sir, K-9 and ordnance teams are still unavailable."

Rich scowled. "Did they say for how long?"

The hulk relayed the question, then his lips flattened after a moment. "They can't break away." Cold eyes flicked at Ian and Natasha before landing on Rich. "The other *situation* has grown worse." He paused as if weighing his words. "They're requesting more help, so I don't see any-one else filling in for them here."

Worthington's scowl deepened. He scanned the envi-ronment, then stilled, his gaze stuck on Lexi. Control Pole Guy had allowed her to climb the hill with the rest of them but kept her off to the side.

Natasha straightened, seeming to understand some-thing Ian didn't.

"Officer Greene." Rich shifted his gaze to her. "Exigent circumstances force me to request your help. Will you and Lexi lead our team through the bombs to the hideout?"

Chapter Thirty-Five

Randy broke from the tree line and crept to his abandoned four-wheeler. He'd managed to stay ahead of Pasha and used the forest to hide. Though, his wanderings had long ago stopped focusing on evading and became driven by figuring out where he was. He'd gotten turned around and never thought he'd find the clearing again.

Now that he had his bearings, he needed to stop running and turn the tables. To do that, he had to have his satellite phone.

Keeping low, he pushed through the tall vegetation. Pasha or one of the other Russians could be lurking in the area, waiting to take a shot. His skin rippled as he ducked even lower into his crouch.

He planned to make two calls. One to his father to explain the Russian's deceit and the second to the FBI—

He gaped at the ATV. Pasha had stolen everything Randy had brought to Alaska and sabotaged the motor.

Randy whirled and ran for the trees. He had no food, water, or phone to call for help. All he had was a determination to survive. And exact revenge.

Ian followed directly behind Natasha in the forest. Twice he tried to increase his pace to walk beside her, but Worthington made it impossible.

Lexi led a motley group. Natasha and Rich were second. The paramedic and Ian were next—she kept supplying him and Natasha with water and power bars—then an assortment of SWAT and CSI techs marched behind, including Doyle. He felt sorry for the one SWAT guy trekking in the bomb suit, sans helmet for the moment. All the various protections built into the olive green, full-body suit had it weighing over seventy unforgiving pounds.

Without the formal unit, Rich had to rely on a recent military-retired EOD specialist—explosive ordnance disposal—to take on the role.

Ian sent up a prayer—something he found easier and easier to do lately—for the specialist. The guy had his work cut out for him if Rich expected him to deactivate all the buried bombs.

Thanks to the food and water breaking the horrible Alaskan-wilderness diet, the fog cleared from Ian's mind and his body was stronger.

God, how do I fix this? His prayer covered too much. Too many things had gone wrong, and most were out of his hands, but he had a slim chance to work on one mistake.

"Nat."

Her spine stiffened, but she didn't verbally respond.

Ahead, Lexi trotted through the evergreens, free of the muzzle.

Ian darted forward, taking the space on Natasha's other side. "Nat, listen to me."

Flashing hazel eyes skewered him, then returned to Lexi. At first, he didn't think she was going to say anything, but she finally asked, "Why…smuggler?"

His throat constricted. He couldn't interpret her belief from those two words. Did she think he was guilty or was she asking him to tell her about the investigation?

Worthington slowed until he walked beside Doyle and

was now right behind them. "I read the file the task force compiled on you, Mr. Dalton."

Ian had trouble swallowing. How thick was it? Worrying about that derailed his need to explain to Natasha. "Like I said before, I worked construction full time, but in my spare hours I contracted with a few companies to fly shipments along the eastern seaboard."

They wended through a section of swaying Black Cottonwood branches encroaching in the already-tight space.

"For one of those companies," Rich interrupted again, "the shipments contained more than just bicycle parts and supplies, didn't they." He wasn't asking.

"That's what I'm told." Ian plucked his hat off and swiped his hand over his matted hair. "It's not true." The urge to place his hat on Natasha's head hit him hard. Not only would it help her with the vegetation, it would signify they were going to be okay.

He'd thought he loved his ex-fiancée, but after meeting Natasha, he realized he hadn't. He'd been grateful the sophisticated woman had chosen him. The entire time he attempted to live up to a standard that never fit him. One second in Natasha's presence and his soul connected to its other half.

"What...?" She swallowed and glanced at him, then back to the dog. "In shipments?"

Ian's stomach tightened. Again, he couldn't interpret Natasha's thoughts. "Stolen paintings, jewelry, and high-end items." The list coated his tongue in ash.

"What Mr. Dalton has failed to mention," Worthington intoned, "is the task force believes he's the prime member of the scheme."

"I'm not."

"They surmise," Rich barreled on, "he willingly flew the stolen items—"

"I never knew they were in the shipments!" Ian exploded, wishing someone would believe him for once.

Rich raised an eyebrow. "But you can't prove you didn't."

Ian whirled. "You can't prove I *did*."

"And that's the crux." Worthington shrugged. "Their forensic accountants haven't found a trace of payments anywhere."

Ian sighed, defeated. He was tired of saying the same things over and over. "Because there is *no* money to trace. I'm not smuggling anything. I never have and never will."

Natasha peered at him, her expression unreadable.

He placed a careful hand on her bicep, and the hard cast beneath the layers met his fingers. "I certainly never invited Randy Puckett or the Russian Mafia here to establish an international smuggling empire." She hadn't shaken him off yet. "And I *know* you didn't transport bomb parts in your luggage."

Lexi alerted, robbing Ian of a response.

Law enforcement monopolized Natasha and Lexi's attention. Ian found himself at the back of the group. Bomb Suit Guy took over, and under his direction, crime scene tape was strung to mark a safe passage. One of the CSI techs took a second roll and headed back to the ravine so everyone would know where to safely begin walking. Bomb Suit also tied pieces of tape to trees near buried bombs.

Lexi identified the explosives, but she focused on finding the hideout, not traversing the entire area. Another K-9 and ordnance team would eventually have to clear the forest. Soon. An animal could set a bomb off and start a fire. With all the trees and shrubs, it would rage out of control fast.

The space around the cleverly hidden hideout quickly ran out of room. Bomb Suit forced everyone to remain as far back as they could. With the buried explosives still active, that meant clumps of people congregated throughout. The boggy ground hadn't had time to dry, so those not wearing rugged boots suffered.

Worthington and Doyle prioritized uncovering the device rigged to the cabin over deactivating the land mines. No one knew if Randy had added a timer on top of the threshold trigger.

Just the thought made Ian want to snatch Natasha and Lexi and charge back to the ravine. Even there, he wasn't sure they'd be safe from flying shrapnel.

Lexi wandered away from the commotion, her nose shifting from the ground to the air and back.

Ian eyed Doyle and Worthington. They were deep in conversation with Bomb Suit near the still-flapping back door. The SWAT members closest to him traded stories of other harrowing situations they'd encountered. No one paid attention to him.

Perfect. He eased back, careful to remain in the safe zones. Once he reached where Lexi had disappeared in the trees, he spread the branches and plunged through.

Natasha had the same idea. She popped through two other trees. He opened his mouth to say...something, but she didn't look at him. Just plowed after her partner.

Air seized in his lungs as pain sliced his heart. It couldn't be over. Not yet. He'd made a mistake. Yes, a big one, but he needed a second chance. He'd forgiven her when she'd left out important details, and now he prayed she'd do the same for him.

Please, God, let her forgive me.

Tromping after the two most important females in his life—sorry, Mom—he reflected on how far he'd come to reconnecting with faith. He wasn't all the way there yet, but he no longer felt abandoned.

Lexi slowed at a weird section.

Ian halted beside Natasha, trying to put his finger on

what was wrong. Immense black spruces swayed in the wind, but they didn't look right. "What am I seeing?" He motioned with his hand. "Or not seeing?"

Natasha's frown deepened as she stared at the space.

Lexi continued sniffing. Her snout lifted as she inhaled whatever caught her attention in the air. Craning her neck, she peered back at Natasha, then faced forward.

Natasha closed the distance with Ian on her heels. "Oh," she breathed, reaching her good hand forward. "Camouflage."

The second she said the word, it clicked. The Russians had utilized tightly woven netting made to look like the rest of the environment.

She gripped the fabric and tugged.

Ian did the same. The thin, oversize barrier crumpled, gathering onto the ground.

"Look."

Ian gaped. They had found the "garage." Three cloth-covered lumps highlighted the empty spaces where the ATV's had been stored. Their canvas tarps were heaped nearby. Toolboxes were scattered on the ground, along with an air compressor that hadn't been new twenty years ago.

Lexi bound into the large, excavated space, sniffing everything.

Natasha headed directly toward one of three canvas-covered lumps.

Trepidation curled in his gut. She had two reasons to investigate the remaining equipment. One, curiosity. Two, she planned to go after Randy and finish what she'd started.

He prayed for the first, but knew it was the second.

Whoosh. Dust and dirt clogged the air as she tossed the canvas aside. Another four-wheeler. Well, a skeleton of one. It had been scavenged for parts.

She raced to the next and pulled the canvas.

He ripped off the last one.

Two more ATVs, just like the others, though these didn't look like they would run for long. Multicolored fenders were deeply scratched and broken in places, and they reeked of oil and gas.

He checked the ground. Yep. They were leaking fluids.

Natasha hopped on the closest and twisted to throw her leg over the seat. Determined hazel eyes met his. "I'm going after Randy."

He knew it. His gut clenched. "You can't drive." He pointed at her sling. "Gas is on the right handle grip."

Her chin jutted.

"I'm going to regret this," he muttered, turning his hat backward. He'd do anything for her, including chasing a bomb maker in the middle of an FBI investigation. He was totally gone for this woman. "Shift back. I'll drive."

She did.

While he settled on the seat and oriented himself to the ATV, Natasha had Lexi sniff oil and gas.

"Seek, fast."

Lexi put her nose down and began sniffing.

Ian started the ATV. It rumbled and choked, sputtering. Black smoke plumed from the tailpipe, then cleared.

He coughed, driving into the thick of it as he turned in the tight space. Once he reached the opening, he kept his eyes zeroed on Lexi's tail. They weren't clear of the buried bombs yet.

Following the same direction Randy and company had gone, they passed near the hideout. A cry went up as people scrambled into and out of their way.

"Greene," Worthington thundered. "Dalton, halt."

Doyle ran toward them, his assault rifle not aimed. Yet.

"Follow us," Natasha tried to yell but barely whispered.

"Follow us," Ian repeated. "We're not escaping. We're going after Randy." Unable to linger for fear of Doyle

catching up, Ian twisted his wrist. The ATV jerked forward with another belch of smoke.

Natasha threw her arm around his waist, her sling digging into his lower back.

"There's another ATV," Ian bellowed back at Worthington and Doyle. He did what he could for law enforcement.
It was time for Natasha to find closure.

Chapter Thirty-Six

Natasha clung to Ian. Between the uneven ground and all the twisty turns, she'd be amazed if she didn't fly off the back.

Lexi led the way. She couldn't run as fast anymore, but she kept a steady pace.

They had cleared the buried-bomb area and were now charging into unknown landscape.

This was the third worst mistake of Natasha's life. The first was running into the rigged vestibule. Second was flying into the untamed Alaska wilderness with no backup or authority. And now, the third, escaping FBI custody—though she and Ian weren't formally charged—to chase after Randy.

If she didn't wind up in jail after this, she'd be amazed if she kept her job. Her therapist was going to have a field day when she found out about her Alaskan adventure.

Ian ran over a partially buried dead limb.

She tightened her grip. Another shot of his masculine scent filled her nose, and she loved and hated it. Since the FBI showed up, her emotions had swung from anger to hurt to confusion. After everything they'd experienced together, he purposefully chose not to confide in her. She'd laid her soul bare. Twice. Fell apart in his arms, something she'd never done with *anyone* before, and he didn't reciprocate. Not that she expected him to cry. Just share. Show her he was falling as hard for her as she was for him.

He helped her realize she sought revenge, not justice. He weathered a PTSD episode and not once treated her as weak, even with her injuries and flashbacks. Why didn't he trust she'd do the same for him?

For the same reason you didn't tell him everything in the beginning, her conscience answered. Fine. But that was the beginning. They had connected and grown together. Or at least she thought they had. Her soul recognized him, but did his link to hers? She couldn't declare him definitively innocent, but her heart refused to believe he knew about the stolen merchandise in the shipments. He should've given her a chance to hear about the investigation from him.

A second engine rumbling had her craning to see over her shoulder.

Doyle and Worthington had found the other ATV.

She exhaled, relief easing the knot in her gut. Randy Puckett was a cunning criminal who wouldn't go down without a fight. She and Ian were near the end of their endurance. The constant supply of water and energy bars helped tremendously, but they didn't cure everything.

Her issue with swallowing pride in this instance had vanished, now that Ian had opened her eyes to her true intentions. It didn't matter anymore if *she* placed a pair of handcuffs on Randy. As long as he went to jail, she had closure.

Doyle waited for a large enough space to roar up beside them. His ATV spewed black smoke and sputtered.

"Officer Greene," Rich yelled, fury filling his tanned face. "You have no authority in Alaska. Stop now."

She squeezed Ian. Her voice wouldn't support shouting.

Ian drifted to a stop. "Lexi."

The dog halted, remaining paces ahead. She turned to watch the humans.

Doyle angled the ATV to stop a few feet away from theirs. The machine was vibrating so intensely her teeth almost rattled.

Natasha pushed past her aching throat, "We weren't doing anything but standing around waiting."

"I'm not done talking to you." Worthington's brown eyes sparked.

"Randy is getting away," Natasha retorted. "Help us."

"Doesn't the bomb guy have to deactivate the triggers on the hideout and check for more?" Ian asked. "That takes time."

The urge to kiss him hit hard. Ian had all but trembled since the helicopters appeared, obviously not a fan of law enforcement, for a good reason. The fact that he argued in her favor, even though her latest stunt was reckless, sliced through some of the anger.

"Once you have Randy," Ian continued, "you'll see he set us up. We have *nothing* to do with him."

"Follow Lexi." Natasha pointed. "The rest of—" she cleared her flaming throat "—the team can work the hideout."

Rich's lips flattened and he exchanged a look with Doyle. The silent exchanged seemed to go her way. Doyle nodded once.

"Lexi," Natasha called hoarsely. "Seek, fast."

The German shepherd immediately began trotting again.

Ian allowed Doyle to go next with their ATV, then fell in behind the FBI agents.

Smart. No need to rile things more than they had. She respected ASAC Worthington. The man had been thrown into the middle of a volatile situation with no warning. One of the Ten Most Wanted in the country emailed a video out of the blue, telling the FBI that a meeting between himself, Russian Mafia, a potential smuggler, and a rogue police officer was happening in their backyard. Rich had been called in from whatever plans he had today and told to handle it. Whatever the other "situation" was that tied up resources had to be a doozy.

In very little time, Rich read files, talked to her superior and a task force, and coordinated with specialists to converge on a remote place. He had a right to be cranky and press for answers.

Now he allowed her to continue her pursuit and participated with only a few grumbles. *Respect.*

Lexi slowed and Natasha noticed the light ahead was much brighter. The dog took another few steps, then lay on her belly.

Doyle held up a closed fist.

"Stop," Natasha interpreted for Ian, in case he wasn't familiar with the signal.

The ATV halted and the engine ceased—whether on its own or not was another matter.

Rich and Doyle climbed off their four-wheeler. Worthington motioned for Natasha and Ian to stay.

Snort. And just a moment ago, she'd brimmed with respect. Now annoyance reigned. She wasn't a pet. And she wasn't missing Randy's capture.

The FBI agents skulked to the clearing. Once they slipped beyond the tree line, she struggled off the ATV.

"Nat?" Ian scrambled to her side. "We're supposed to—"

He cut himself off at her look.

"Yeah. The silent command rankled me too."

They hustled forward.

Adrenaline or finally seeing the end in sight pumped energy into her cells. She easily kept up with Ian. Lexi ran with them after they passed her.

The sun blazed overhead. Doyle and Rich examined an abandoned ATV not far into the tall weeds and scrub. A tamped-down area nearby caught her attention. Lexi headed for it as if reading Natasha's mind. She sniffed the broken twigs, then lay on her belly.

"She's caught his scent." Ian pointed.

Doyle and Rich studied the new area.

Lexi bound to her feet, staring behind them. *"Grrrrrr-roooooowwwwwllll."*

Natasha whirled.

An ATV engine sputtered to life.

"NO." Natasha bolted for the forest, ignoring her wailing injuries.

Lexi raced past her.

"Nat!" Ian's footsteps pounded the earth.

Branches smacked into her. She pushed past them. Randy could not escape again.

"Woof. Woof. Woof."

"Freeze," Rich bellowed, surpassing Natasha. Doyle quickly overtook her too.

Randy stomped Doyle's four-wheeler into gear and jerked the ATV forward. Black smoke plumed.

"No. No. No." Her lungs wheezed and her body protested the jostling activity.

Bam. Bam. Bam. Bullets from Doyle's assault rifle tore through the tires.

The ATV lurched, then leaned as the air deflated. Randy cried out.

Lexi soared into the air and smashed into the bomb maker's side. He toppled onto the ground with the German shepherd landing on top.

Before Randy could do more than scream at Lexi's growl, Rich and Doyle surrounded him with weapons aimed.

"Randy Puckett, you're under arrest." Worthington uttered the five sweetest words of the day.

* * *

Ian combed his fingers through his still-wet, but clean, hair. The Anchorage hospital had allowed him to use the shower in an empty patient room. They couldn't do anything about his filthy clothing, but he managed to find a pair of sweatpants and a T-shirt in the lost-and-found bin.

"You're free to go."

Ian snapped his gaze up to find ASAC Rich Worthington hovering in the doorway. Hope sprouted inside and he had to swallow twice before he could speak. "Do you mean the hospital or your custody?" He had to make sure he understood.

Half of Rich's mouth twitched up. "My custody."

Black spots crowded Ian's vision. The past five hours had been filled with examinations, tests, bloodwork, IVs, and medications. His concussion was on the mend, and the doctors couldn't do much for bruised ribs. With all the drugs in his system, the elation expounded.

"We don't have everything back from the lab yet." Rich wiped at a streak of dirt on his coat. "But the preliminary results support your story. There are bullet holes all through the fuselage, your radio was destroyed, we haven't found a single fingerprint of yours inside the cabin, and there's not a single phone record showing you contacting Puckett or the Russian Mafia. There's also nothing indicating you paid for a phone to hide that activity."

A sloppy grin filled his face. "Does this mean the smuggling investigation's over?"

"No." Rich straightened. "That's still underway." He scratched the beginnings of a beard, his skin showing signs of exhaustion. "I'm not at liberty to elaborate on this, but the task force may have found a second pilot transporting stolen goods hidden in legitimate shipments."

"Really?" The elation tripled. Now the investigators

would see he'd been a victim duped into smuggling their merchandise.

"That doesn't mean you're off the hook." Rich pointed a finger at him. "But, it's something."

"Do you know if Officer Greene is still in the hospital?"

Rich shook his head. "She's gone. Internal Affairs summoned her back to Philadelphia."

"No." Ian stood, then swayed. His brain wasn't keeping up with his movements. "She can't leave yet."

"Slow down." Rich held up his hands. "You can't catch her."

"Want to bet." Ian blinked against the fresh round of spots.

"Ian." Rich's soft voice had him pausing. "Stop. Let the doctors discharge you properly, then come up with a plan." He paused. "I'm not looking to intrude on your personal life, but it's obvious you didn't tell her about the investigation." He swished his hand. "No need to explain. A flashing neon sign would be less noticeable than the hangdog expressions and heart-eyes. You've fallen for the woman and got tongue-tied when it came to telling her about the task force. Just…" He scratched the back of his neck. "If you're going to apologize, make it count. Use this time to figure out what to say, then grovel like a champion."

Ian blinked. The hard-as-nails agent had just given him excellent advice on his love life. Wow. Was this a dream?

Rich dropped his hand. "Believe it or not—" he met Ian's gaze "—I hope you succeed in gaining her forgiveness and being dismissed from the investigation. I've added my two cents to your file. Hope it helps."

ASAC Worthington pivoted and walked out the door, leaving Ian with his mouth wide open.

"From your lips to God's ears," Ian managed to mutter, then began planning his trip to Philadelphia.

Chapter Thirty-Seven

Natasha settled her left hand between Lexi's ears.

"Officer Greene." The Internal Affairs woman leaned against the wooden desk piled with files and paper. "Are you sure this is what you want?"

"Natasha." Lieutenant Aydem turned in the visitor chair beside her. "You don't have to do this. Take time off. Heal. And talk to me when you're ready to come back."

Scratching her partner's fur, Natasha drew strength from the amazing dog. "It's the right thing to do," she rasped, her voice still not healed.

It had been two days since she landed in Philadelphia, though her body couldn't tell, thanks to all the time differences and dreaded layovers.

Yesterday, she'd barely left the police station. Between meetings with her superiors and Internal Affairs, she hadn't had a moment to herself. Leaving the state without Lieutenant Aydem's permission landed a disciplinary action in her file. Another disciplinary action sat beside the first for investigating after being specifically ordered not to. She would've had a third for the mess in Alaska, but thankfully that was cleared up. At least for her. Worthington wouldn't say anything about Ian, but he did let her know HRT intercepted a plane attempting to pick up four

Russian men. Those men and the pilot were taken into custody.

"An officer should never allow her job to become personal." Natasha ducked her head, embarrassed at her actions. "My conduct almost cost Lexi her life." A hitch caught in her throat and she had to take a minute to keep her composure. "I almost cost a civilian his life too." Ian Dalton's face drifted through her mind. Her heart panged. They had been through so much, yet had so little time together.

"Natasha." Lieutenant Aydem's wrinkled face peered at her with sorrow. "Don't leave."

"I have to," she whispered, her rasp giving out. "I'm not fit to wear the badge anymore."

Those words stabbed her weeping soul. She'd given so much of herself for this job, but it was time to move on. God had something else planned for her. She had to trust Him to show her.

Wobbling to her feet, she unclipped her badge and placed it on top of a file stack, then did the same for the gun holstered at her side.

Ian shifted on the hot concrete steps. August in Philadelphia came with high heat and humidity. Sweat dripped down his cheeks and he swiped the rivulets. If Natasha didn't leave the station soon, he'd melt before he had a chance to talk to her.

Maybe he should've rethought the freshly pressed khaki pants and button-down shirt. Sun baked the front steps and he had no way to avoid it. Shade didn't—

The front doors swished open again blasting him with a shot of cold air-conditioning. Ian peered over his shoulder and froze.

Natasha strode through with Lexi at her side.

His heart jumped into his throat and he couldn't swallow. He'd never missed a woman and her dog so much. If he hadn't already figured it out, he'd know at this very moment that Natasha was his soulmate. And Lexi had a permanent home in his heart.

Drooped shoulders, dark circles under her eyes, and wrinkled suit announced Natasha's exhaustion. He couldn't imagine an Internal Affairs interrogation, but her body language said it wasn't pleasant. The urge to gather her in his arms raged strong. He needed to hold her for too many reasons.

"Woof." Lexi trotted down three steps and jammed her nose against Ian's cheek. A sloppy, wet lick followed and Ian laughed.

Throwing his arms around the K-9, he hugged her against him. "I missed you too."

"Ian?"

His muscles twitched at Natasha's hoarse voice. He hated for her that it hadn't healed yet.

"Time to face the music," he whispered into one of Lexi's tall ears.

The German shepherd panted as she stepped back to allow him to stand.

"Nat, um. Hi." *Way to bowl her over.* Remember the speech. His mind blanked. Lost in her beautiful hazel eyes, every word he'd practiced disappeared.

"Ian?" Her guarded features gave him no indication how she felt.

"I, um." He scratched the back of his newly barbered hair. "I was hoping we could talk." *Hooray! A full sentence.*

The doors swished again, and an older man in a full uniform strode through. "Natasha."

She turned. "Sir."

The older man waved an arm. "I talked to IA. We're giving you a leave of absence."

"But—"

"You need time to process everything," the man continued, closing the distance. "Don't make any decisions now. Please. I've locked your gun and badge in my safe. They'll be waiting for you when you're ready."

"But—"

"You're too good of an officer." His brown face softened. "I can't lose you. The city can't lose you. Take the time you need." His gaze slid to Ian and stuck. "Can I help you?"

"Oh, um," Ian stammered brilliantly. He was on a roll right now.

"Lieutenant Aydem—" Natasha motioned with her hand "—meet Ian Dalton."

"The pilot from Alaska?" Brown eyes assessed him shrewdly. "You're a long way from the wilderness. Did you get lost?"

"No, I…" Ian cleared his throat. "…wanted to talk to Nat."

"Nat?" Graying eyebrows flew upward. "You're still alive after calling her that?" He whistled. "You must be someone special."

Pink bloomed across Natasha's cheeks. "Standing right here."

"We see you." Lieutenant Aydem winked at Ian. "All the best with your talk, Ian." The man pivoted and marched back inside.

"You quit?" Ian climbed to her step.

Her eyebrows drew down. "I guess I'm on a leave of absence."

Ian exhaled. "Good. You can't quit. You're too good of an officer."

"How would you know?" The guarded expression took over again.

"I saw you in action." He risked moving closer. Only three feet separated them.

"What are you doing here, Ian?" She shook her head. "Sorry, that came out wrong. It's been a long two days. I'm functioning on will power and caffeine." She rubbed her forehead. "Are you okay? Nothing broken or permanently damaged?"

Every cell in his body tried to leap forward to hold her. Cradle her. Give her a place to shelter. "I'm fine." Another foot closer. "And you? Are you okay?" He wanted to know everything.

She nodded. "I'm fine. My bones are still healing, and my concussion is being monitored by daily calls with my personal physician."

"Excellent." His speech dried on his tongue. How did he begin?

She bit her lip and he finally saw the first sign of her guarded exterior cracking. Hurt and confusion swam in her hazel irises. "I don't mean to be rude, but why did you come here?"

"I came here for you." His heart pounded against his ribs. "I'm sorry." The sentiment wasn't enough.

Her breath hitched. "For what?"

"Everything." He poured his regret into the word. "But let's start with the smuggling investigation. I should've told you about it."

Pain flashed across her face and it gutted him.

"You gave me a precious gift." His fingers lifted to touch her but he stopped short. "You gave me your pain, your suffering, your burdens. But I wasn't strong enough to do the same and it hurt us both. I'm sorry. You'll never realize how much I regret not confiding in you." He rubbed his trimmed beard. "I kept thinking I had more time. And fear whispered how you wouldn't believe I was innocent." He exhaled and slumped. "I was wrong about so much."

Lexi bumped his thigh. He dug his fingers into the fur near her ears.

"Nat." He halved the space between them. Her scent filled his terrified soul. "I never want to let you go." Blood thundered in his veins. He was putting everything out there. "From the first moment I saw you, I knew my life would never be the same. It didn't take long for me to realize what that meant. You're my other half."

"Ian." She grazed his cheek and he wanted to weep at the caress. "I wish you'd trusted me. It hurts that you assumed the worst."

He couldn't stop his palm from pressing her hand against his face. "I wish I had too." He tilted his head to hug her hand. "My cowardice was all about *me*, not you. I *do* trust you, Nat. I've given you my heart."

Her pupils widened.

"I want to share everything and anything you want to know. Nothing held back. Please give me a chance. Give *us* a chance."

"Ian," she whispered. "You've had my heart all along."

Elation tore through the terror. "I did? I do?"

She nodded. "God led me to you. I hadn't wanted to believe it at first, but it didn't take long for me to realize you held the other half of my soul."

The biggest, sloppiest grin split his lips and he whooped.

Two uniformed police officers paused climbing the steps. Huge smiles broke over their faces as they shook their heads and kept going.

Resting his forehead against hers, he whispered, "Nat, I promise you I'm innocent of the smuggling charge."

"I never had a doubt, Ace."

* * * * *

Get 4 FREE REWARDS!

We'll send you 2 FREE Books plus 2 FREE Mystery Gifts.

FREE
Value Over
$20

Both the **Love Inspired®** and **Love Inspired® Suspense** series feature compelling novels filled with inspirational romance, faith, forgiveness and hope.

YES! Please send me 2 FREE novels from the Love Inspired or Love Inspired Suspense series and my 2 FREE gifts (gifts are worth about $10 retail). After receiving them, if I don't wish to receive any more books, I can return the shipping statement marked "cancel." If I don't cancel, I will receive 6 brand-new Love Inspired Larger-Print books or Love Inspired Suspense Larger-Print books every month and be billed just $6.49 each in the U.S. or $6.74 each in Canada. That is a savings of at least 16% off the cover price. It's quite a bargain! Shipping and handling is just 50¢ per book in the U.S. and $1.25 per book in Canada.* I understand that accepting the 2 free books and gifts places me under no obligation to buy anything. I can always return a shipment and cancel at any time by calling the number below. The free books and gifts are mine to keep no matter what I decide.

Choose one: ☐ **Love Inspired**   ☐ **Love Inspired Suspense**
　　　　　　　　Larger-Print　　　　　　　**Larger-Print**
　　　　　　　　(122/322 IDN GRHK)　　　　　(107/307 IDN GRHK)

Name (please print)

Address   Apt. #

City   State/Province   Zip/Postal Code

Email: Please check this box ☐ if you would like to receive newsletters and promotional emails from Harlequin Enterprises ULC and its affiliates. You can unsubscribe anytime.

Mail to the Harlequin Reader Service:
IN U.S.A.: P.O. Box 1341, Buffalo, NY 14240-8531
IN CANADA: P.O. Box 603, Fort Erie, Ontario L2A 5X3

Want to try 2 free books from another series! Call 1-800-873-8635 or visit www.ReaderService.com.

---

*Terms and prices subject to change without notice. Prices do not include sales taxes, which will be charged (if applicable) based on your state or country of residence. Canadian residents will be charged applicable taxes. Offer not valid in Quebec. This offer is limited to one order per household. Books received may not be as shown. Not valid for current subscribers to the Love Inspired or Love Inspired Suspense series. All orders subject to approval. Credit or debit balances in a customer's account(s) may be offset by any other outstanding balance owed by or to the customer. Please allow 4 to 6 weeks for delivery. Offer available while quantities last.

Your Privacy—Your information is being collected by Harlequin Enterprises ULC, operating as Harlequin Reader Service. For a complete summary of the information we collect, how we use this information and to whom it is disclosed, please visit our privacy notice located at corporate.harlequin.com/privacy-notice. From time to time we may also exchange your personal information with reputable third parties. If you wish to opt out of this sharing of your personal information, please visit readerservice.com/consumerschoice or call 1-800-873-8635. **Notice to California Residents**—Under California law, you have specific rights to control and access your data. For more information on these rights and how to exercise them, visit corporate.harlequin.com/california-privacy.

LIRLIS22R3

Get 4 FREE REWARDS!

We'll send you 2 FREE Books plus 2 FREE Mystery Gifts.

FREE
Value Over
$20

Both the **Harlequin® Special Edition** and **Harlequin® Heartwarming™** series feature compelling novels filled with stories of love and strength where the bonds of friendship, family and community unite.